QUANTUM MECHANICS

QUANTUM MECHANICS

JEFF WEIGEL

CHAPTER 1

Far Rim
SALVAGE & REPAIR

I PULLED THESE THERMOCHARGERS OFF AN *OLDER MODEL* SPEEDER-- THE D40.
THAT RUSTY ONE OVER BY THE GEYSER?
YEAH.

THESE CHARGERS ARE A LITTLE SMALL. I FLARED THE CONNECTORS A BIT WITH YOUR DAD'S SPANNERS SO THEY'D FIT.
IT'S WORTH A TRY, ANYWAY.
JEEZ, THESE NEUTRON FILTERS ARE A MESS!

SHOULD BE OKAY--'LESS THERE'S INTERIOR CORROSION. WE WON'T KNOW FOR SURE UNTIL WE START IT UP.
IT'LL WORK! YOU GOTTA HAVE CONFIDENCE, ZAM!

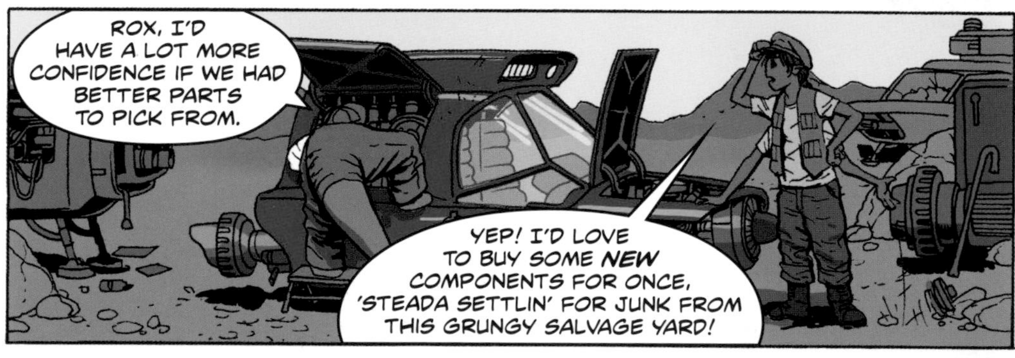
ROX, I'D HAVE A LOT MORE CONFIDENCE IF WE HAD BETTER PARTS TO PICK FROM.
YEP! I'D LOVE TO BUY SOME *NEW* COMPONENTS FOR ONCE, 'STEADA SETTLIN' FOR JUNK FROM THIS GRUNGY SALVAGE YARD!

THESE PARTS MAY BE OLD, BUT THIS IS STILL THE GREATEST *TOY STORE* IN THE WHOLE SYSTEM!
IF YOU LIKE DIRTY, RUSTY, BROKEN-DOWN OLD TOYS!

WELL, I DO!
CRANK IT OVER-- LET'S SEE HOW WE DID!
HERE GOES--!
RRRR RRRR RRRR

KABANG!
THAT CAN'T BE RIGHT!
IT'S NOT! ABANDON SHIP!

FWOOSH!

BA-DOOM

YEP. CORROSION ON THE THERMOCHARGERS, ALL RIGHT.
WELL, THAT'S JUST *GREAT!*

NOW WHAT DO WE DO?! THAT WAS THE LAST SALVAGEABLE SPEEDER ON THIS STUPID ASTEROID!
WELL... THERE'S THAT SHUTTLECRAFT OVER BY THE FREIGHTER--
SHUTTLECRAFT?! THAT'S NOT COOL! A *SPEEDER* WITH A *QUANTUM HYPERDRIVE* IS *COOL!*

BESIDES, ZAM--WE CAN'T EVEN *LIFT* THE PARTS WE'D NEED FOR A BIGGER JOB LIKE THAT SHUTTLE, AND MY DAD WON'T LET US USE THE ROBOTS.

YOUR DAD'S KINDA PROTECTIVE OF THE 'BOTS EVER SINCE WE MELTED HIS TURBOLIFTER.
YEAH. I REALLY THOUGHT IT'D BE TOUGH ENOUGH FOR NUCLEAR WELDING WORK! *OOPS!*

AND THEN HE MADE US CLEAN AND LUBE ALL THOSE JUNKERS TO MAKE UP FOR IT!
THAT WAS *FUN!*
C'MON-- LET'S HEAD BACK TO THE GARAGE. NOT MUCH WE CAN DO HERE NOW.

HI, KIDS! FINISHED FOR THE NIGHT?
I HEARD A LOUD NOISE OVER IN YOUR DIRECTION. WHAT WAS THAT ABOUT?
WE'RE *FINISHED*, ALL RIGHT!
DANG THRUSTER FITTINGS...!

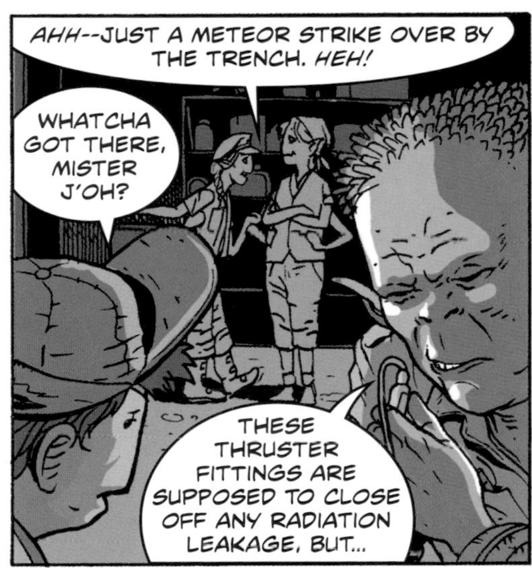
AHH--JUST A METEOR STRIKE OVER BY THE TRENCH. *HEH!*
WHATCHA GOT THERE, MISTER J'OH?
THESE THRUSTER FITTINGS ARE SUPPOSED TO CLOSE OFF ANY RADIATION LEAKAGE, BUT...

LOOKS LIKE THE O-RINGS ARE SHRUNK UP--MAYBE FROM A LIQUID HYDROGEN SPILL?
HMM. COULD BE. LET'S CHECK THIS LINE BY THE--
YEP! THERE IT IS! GOOD CALL, ZAM!
FSSSS

KID, YOU GOT QUITE A KNACK FOR THIS STUFF!
I BEEN STUDYIN' UP ON NUCLEAR THRUSTERS IN THOSE SHOP MANUALS YOU LET ME BORROW.
WHAT A *NERD!*

I WAS GONNA TRY OUT SOME OF WHAT I LEARNED ON THE OLD SPEEDER ROX AND I ARE WORKIN' ON, BUT--
PULEEZE, ROX! WE'RE NOT DUMB.
AHEM! HEY, ZAM-- THAT WAS QUITE A METEOR STRIKE WE SAW, WASN'T IT!
YOUR MOM AND I CAN HEAR THE DIFFERENCE BETWEEN A METEOR STRIKE AND AN ENGINE EXPLODIN', ROX.

SORRY--THAT WAS MY FAULT, MR. J'OH. SHOULDN'T 'A TRUSTED THOSE OLD THERMOCHARGERS I FOUND.
I SEE YA GOT SOME OLD POWER CELLS LAYIN' AROUND. MIND IF I--
YOU'RE WELCOME TO TAKE 'EM, ZAM.

HA! WHAT'RE YOU GONNA DO WITH BROKEN-DOWN, OLD POWER CELLS!
ZAM, WOULD YOU LIKE TO STAY FOR DINNER? I'VE GOT IT WARMING UP IN THE GALLEY RIGHT NOW.

NO THANKS, MA'AM. I'M GONNA HEAD BACK TO MY PLACE. I'VE GOT SOME TINKERING TO DO.
UH, OKAY, ZAM. WELL, SEE YA TOMORROW.
SEE YA, ROX.

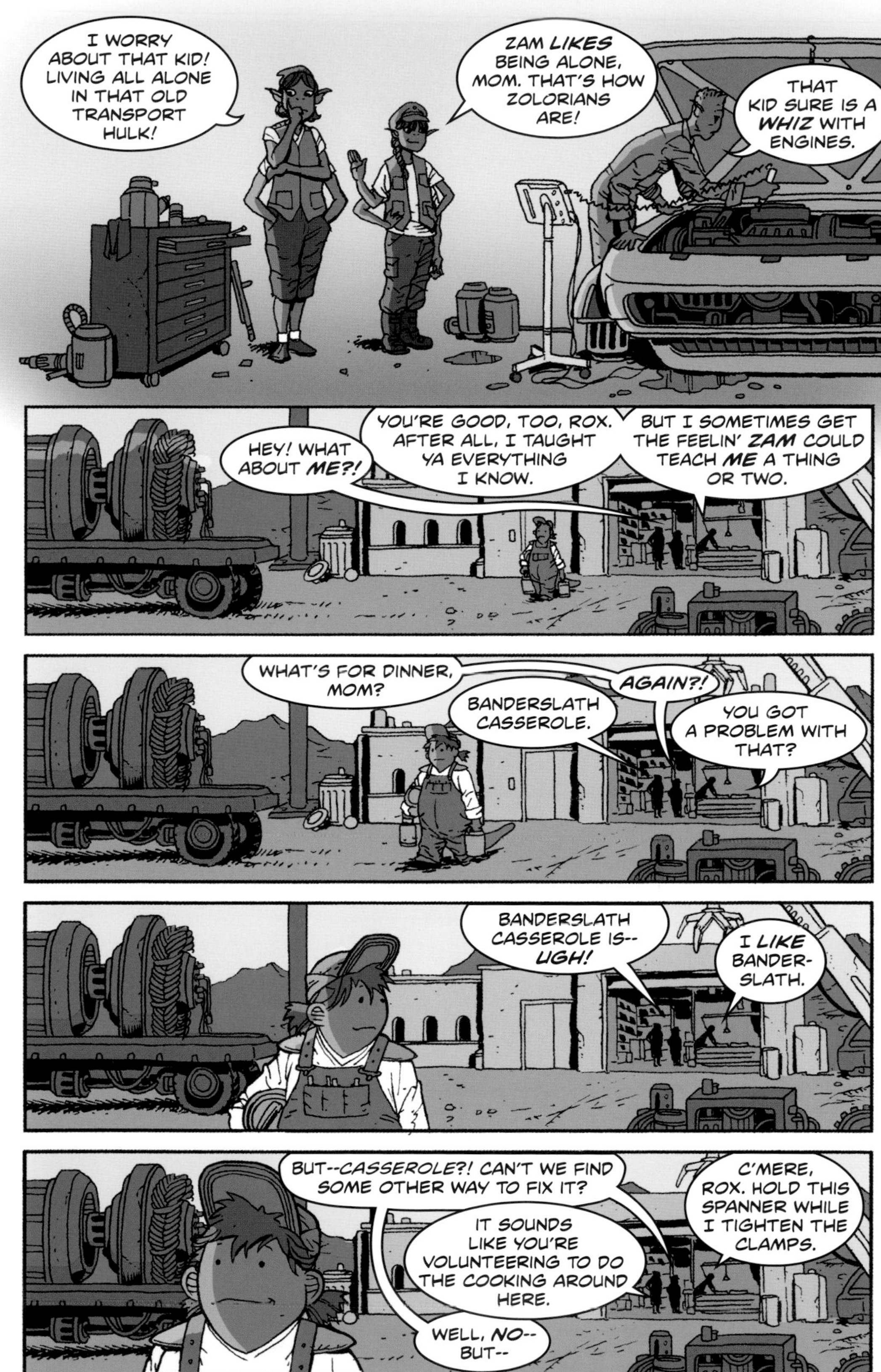
I WORRY ABOUT THAT KID! LIVING ALL ALONE IN THAT OLD TRANSPORT HULK!
ZAM LIKES BEING ALONE, MOM. THAT'S HOW ZOLORIANS ARE!
THAT KID SURE IS A WHIZ WITH ENGINES.
HEY! WHAT ABOUT ME?!
YOU'RE GOOD, TOO, ROX. AFTER ALL, I TAUGHT YA EVERYTHING I KNOW.
BUT I SOMETIMES GET THE FEELIN' ZAM COULD TEACH ME A THING OR TWO.
WHAT'S FOR DINNER, MOM?
BANDERSLATH CASSEROLE.
AGAIN?!
YOU GOT A PROBLEM WITH THAT?
BANDERSLATH CASSEROLE IS-- UGH!
I LIKE BANDER-SLATH.
BUT--CASSEROLE?! CAN'T WE FIND SOME OTHER WAY TO FIX IT?
C'MERE, ROX. HOLD THIS SPANNER WHILE I TIGHTEN THE CLAMPS.
IT SOUNDS LIKE YOU'RE VOLUNTEERING TO DO THE COOKING AROUND HERE.
WELL, NO-- BUT--

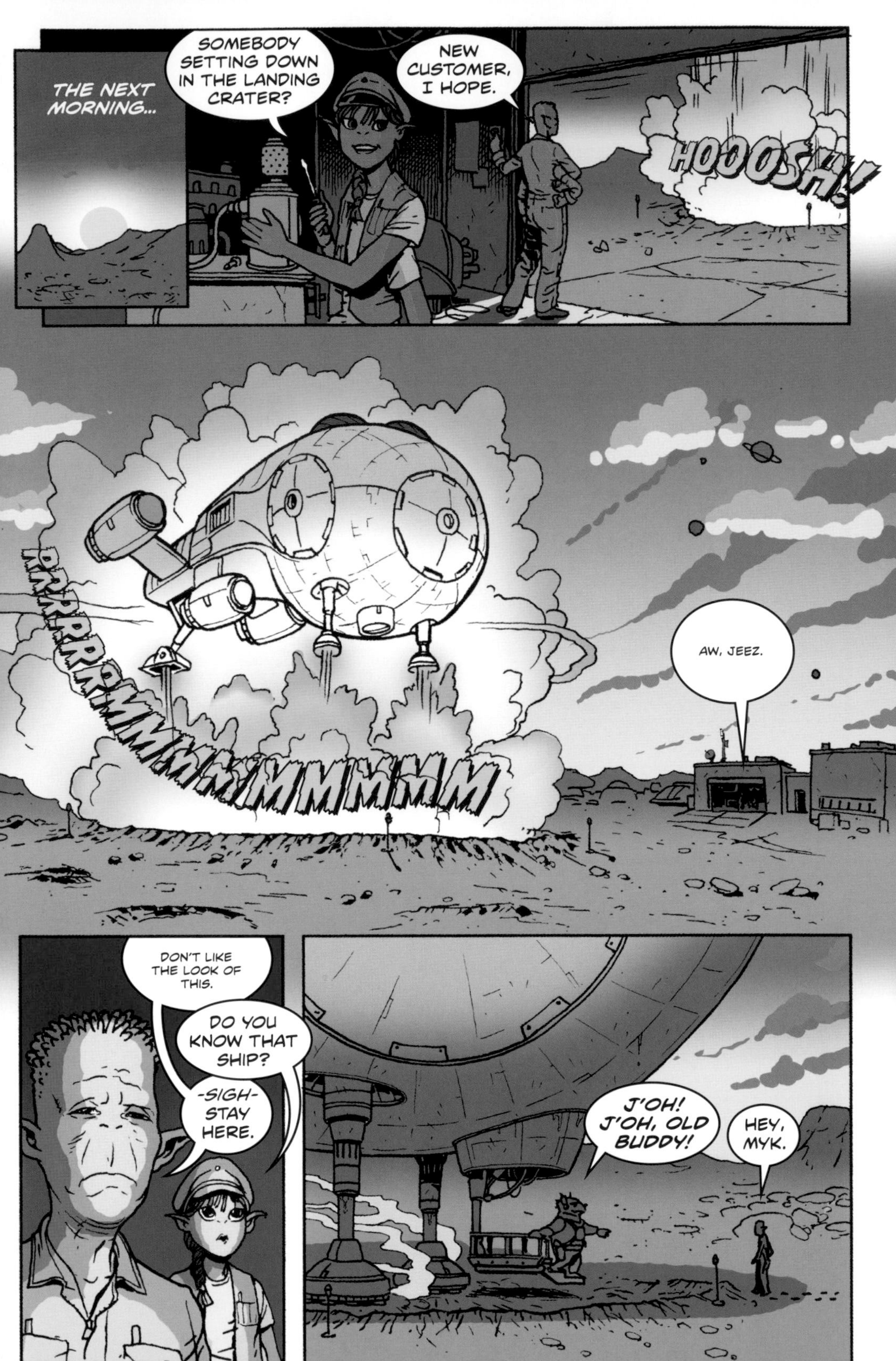
THE NEXT MORNING...
SOMEBODY SETTING DOWN IN THE LANDING CRATER?
NEW CUSTOMER, I HOPE.
HOOOOSH!!
RRRRRRMMMMMMMMMMMM
AW, JEEZ.
DON'T LIKE THE LOOK OF THIS.
DO YOU KNOW THAT SHIP?
-SIGH- STAY HERE.
J'OH! J'OH, OLD BUDDY!
HEY, MYK.

GOOD TO SEE YA AGAIN, J'OH! HOW'S LIFE IN THIS ARMPIT OF A SPACE SECTOR BEEN TREATIN' YA?
UH...OKAY. JUST TRYIN' TO GET ALONG AND MAKE AN HONEST LIVIN'.
HEH! YEAH. YEAH. RIGHT!
J'OH, I GOT SOME WORK FOR YOU, IF YOU'RE INTERESTED.
I DON'T DO YOUR KINDA WORK, MYK.
AW, IT AIN'T LIKE THAT, J'OH! IT'S...
HEY, DAD, CAN I...
WELL, NOW! WHO'S THIS?
ROX, CAN YOU WORK ON PULLIN' THOSE COMPRESSORS APART FOR ME?
UH...WELL, OKAY.
SO LISTEN, J'OH--MY SHIP'S HAVIN' TROUBLE WITH HER TRACTOR BEAM. I KNOW YOU COULD FIX THAT WITH YOUR EYES CLOSED. WHADDAYA SAY?
SORRY, MYK. I'VE GOT MY HANDS PRETTY FULL RIGHT NOW.

C'MON, PAL! FOR OLD TIME'S SAKE JUST COME ABOARD AND TAKE A LOOK. IT'LL HARDLY TAKE YOU ANY TIME AT ALL!
SORRY. I CAN'T HELP YA, MYK.

IT'LL BE JUST LIKE THE OLD DAYS, J'OH-- DON'TCHA WANNA GET YOUR HANDS DIRTY ON A REAL SHIP, 'STEAD OF THESE RUST BUCKETS YOU GOT AROUND HERE?
I DO JUST FINE WITH THESE "RUST BUCKETS."

WELL, WORKIN' ON THE QUASAR TORRENT PAYS A LOT BETTER! ME AND THE CREW HAVE BEEN DOIN' GREAT LATELY, AND...
YEAH, SO I HEAR...

...BUT YOU'LL JUST HAVE TO TAKE YOUR SHIP OVER TO THE CENTAURI SYSTEM IF YOU NEED IT FIXED.
YOU KNOW I CAN'T DO THAT, J'OH.
NOT MY PROBLEM, MYK.

HEY, DAD--
I GOT THIS COMPRESSOR
APART AND...
THAT'S GOOD, ROX. I'M HEADED
OUT INTO THE YARD FOR A BIT. I'LL
BE BACK IN A WHILE.
UH...
OKAY.

HUH!
HOW DO YA LIKE
THAT?
NOW
WHADDA I DO
ABOUT--?
HEY,
MISTER!
WHAT'S UP,
KID?
AH...WELL, I HEARD
MY DAD SAY HE WAS TOO
BUSY TO HELP WITH YOUR
TRACTOR BEAM...
...BUT ME AND
A FRIEND OF MINE ARE
GREAT MECHANICS!
I KNOW *WE* COULD FIX
IT FOR YOU!

HMMF! REALLY?!
YEAH! YEAH! DEFINITELY! MY DAD TAUGHT ME EVERYTHING HE KNOWS, AND--

OKAY, KID. I'LL GIVE YOU A CRACK AT IT. WHAT'VE I GOT TO LOSE?
SWEET! I'LL BE RIGHT BACK!

ZAM!
HEY, ZAM!

WHAT'S UP, ROX?
YOU KNOW HOW I SAID WE NEEDED TO BUY SOME DECENT PARTS AND EQUIPMENT?

WELL, GRAB YOUR TOOL KIT--
WE JUST SCORED A PAYING JOB!

WHAT! HOW!? WHERE?
THERE'S A SHIP IN THE LANDING CRATER THAT NEEDS ITS TRACTOR BEAM FIXED RIGHT AWAY. DAD SAYS HE'S TOO BUSY, BUT I TOLD THE PILOT WE COULD HANDLE IT!
UM-- WE CAN, RIGHT?
TRACTOR BEAM--HUH! I'VE BEEN READING UP ON THOSE, AND...
PERFECT! LET'S GRAB SOME TOOLS!

MAYBE WE COULD USE THIS MONEY TO GET THAT SPEEDER DOWN ON THE SOUTH CORNER OF THE YARD RUNNIN' AGAIN!
AW, YEAH! THAT THING'S JUST ONE PROTON ACCELERATOR AWAY FROM BEIN' SPACEWORTHY!
PLUS MAYBE A NEW TURBO-THRUSTER.
COULD USE SOME NEW SEATS, TOO.

WAIT'LL YOU SEE THIS SHIP WE'RE GONNA BE WORKING ON-- IT'S HUGE!
I BET THAT THING'S BEEN ALL OVER THE GALAXY! BOY, I'D SURE LIKE TO...

READY!
ZAM! YOU CAN'T BRING EVERY TOOL YOU OWN! JUST BRING WHAT YOU THINK YOU'LL NEED!
AWWW!
YOU'LL MAKE US LOOK LIKE AMATEURS! JEEZ!
!
REALLY?

HERE WE ARE, MISTER! THIS IS MY PARTNER, ZAM! WE'LL HAVE YOUR TRACTOR BEAM TOWIN' *WHOLE MOONS* IN NO TIME!

TWO TRACTOR BEAM EXPERTS, EH? LUCKY ME!
I WOULDN'T SAY WE'RE *EXPERTS*...
SURE! WE'VE FIXED *TONS* OF TRACTOR BEAMS!

'COURSE...UH... WE CAN'T GIVE YOU AN ESTIMATE UNTIL WE SEE WHAT THE PROBLEM IS.
OH, I'M SURE YOU'LL BE WORTH EVERY BITCREDIT I PAY YOU!

RED MYK IS BACK, YOU GUYS!
WELCOME ABOARD THE *QUASAR TORRENT*, KIDS. DON'T LET THE CREW SCARE YA!

C'MON! THE ENGINE ROOM'S ON THE OTHER SIDE OF THE SHIP.
WHAT'S WITH THE KIDS, CAP'N?
THEY'RE MECHANICS!
MECHANICS! *THOSE* TWO?!

THIS HERE'S THE GALLEY.
IT'S ...UM... NICE.
KEEP IT DOWN, YOU BUMS! WE GOT GUESTS!
GREAT BUNCHA GUYS. YOU'LL LIKE 'EM.

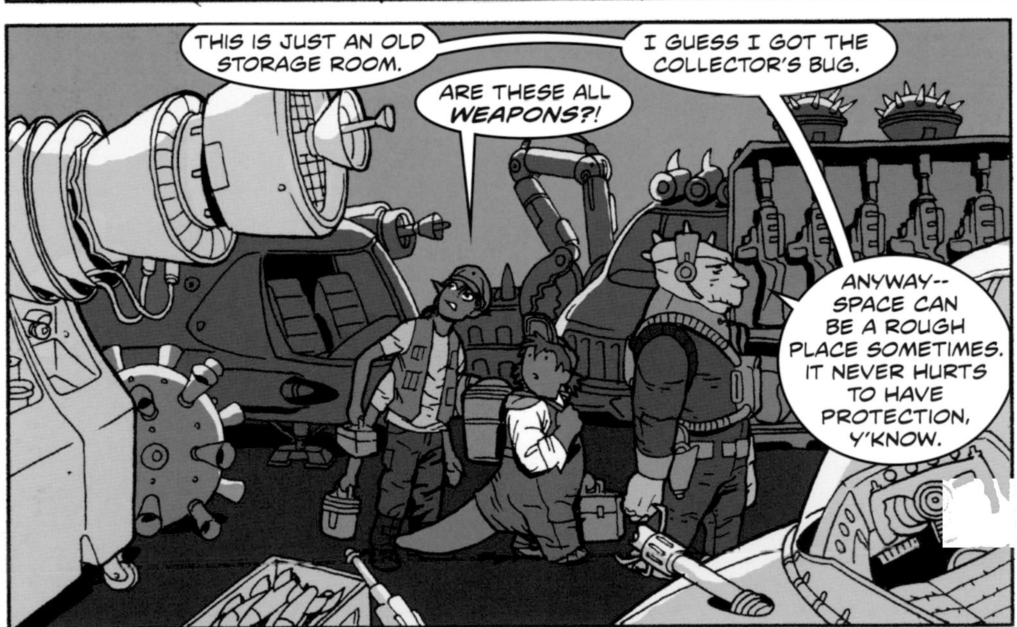
THIS IS JUST AN OLD STORAGE ROOM.
ARE THESE ALL *WEAPONS?!*
I GUESS I GOT THE COLLECTOR'S BUG.
ANYWAY-- SPACE CAN BE A ROUGH PLACE SOMETIMES. IT NEVER HURTS TO HAVE PROTECTION, Y'KNOW.

THIS IS THE MECHANICAL DECK. WE'RE ALMOST THERE.

YUCK!

WATCH YOUR STEP, KID.

SO AIN'T SHE A ***GEM?*** I TELL YA--THE ***QUASAR TORRENT'S*** THE FASTEST QUANTUM RUNNER ON THIS SIDE 'A THE GALAXY!

LUCKY FOR US, TOO!

ER--YEAH! SHE'S A REAL BEAUTY! AND ONCE WE'RE DONE WITH HER, SHE'LL BE IN *PERFECT* WORKING ORDER AGAIN!

IS THAT A ***QUANTUM ACCELERATOR*** OVER THERE?! I'VE NEVER SEEN ONE UP CLOSE BEFORE!

SHH!!!

OUR TRACTOR BEAM IS RIGHT THROUGH HERE.

WE THINK THE RETRACTION COIL IS THE PROBLEM, BUT WE'RE NOT POSITIVE. SEE WHAT YOU CAN MAKE OF IT.
DON'T WORRY, MISTER. WE'LL HAVE IT RUNNING AGAIN IN NO TIME!

I GOT THINGS TO DO, BUT I'LL BE BACK LATER TO CHECK ON YA.

SO...
...EVER SEE ONE OF THESE BEFORE?
UH... NOPE.

WELL, WE WANTED SOMETHING TO WORK ON BESIDES JUNKERS-- THIS IS OUR CHANCE!
RIGHT! ANYWAY-- WHAT'S THE WORST THAT COULD HAPPEN?
THAT'S THE SPIRIT!

HEY-- THAT NOISE! IS THAT THE ENGINES FIRING UP?!

IT SURE IS! WHAT'S GOING ON?!

BBBRRRROOOOOMMMMMMMMMMMM

GAAHH!!

WHOA!!

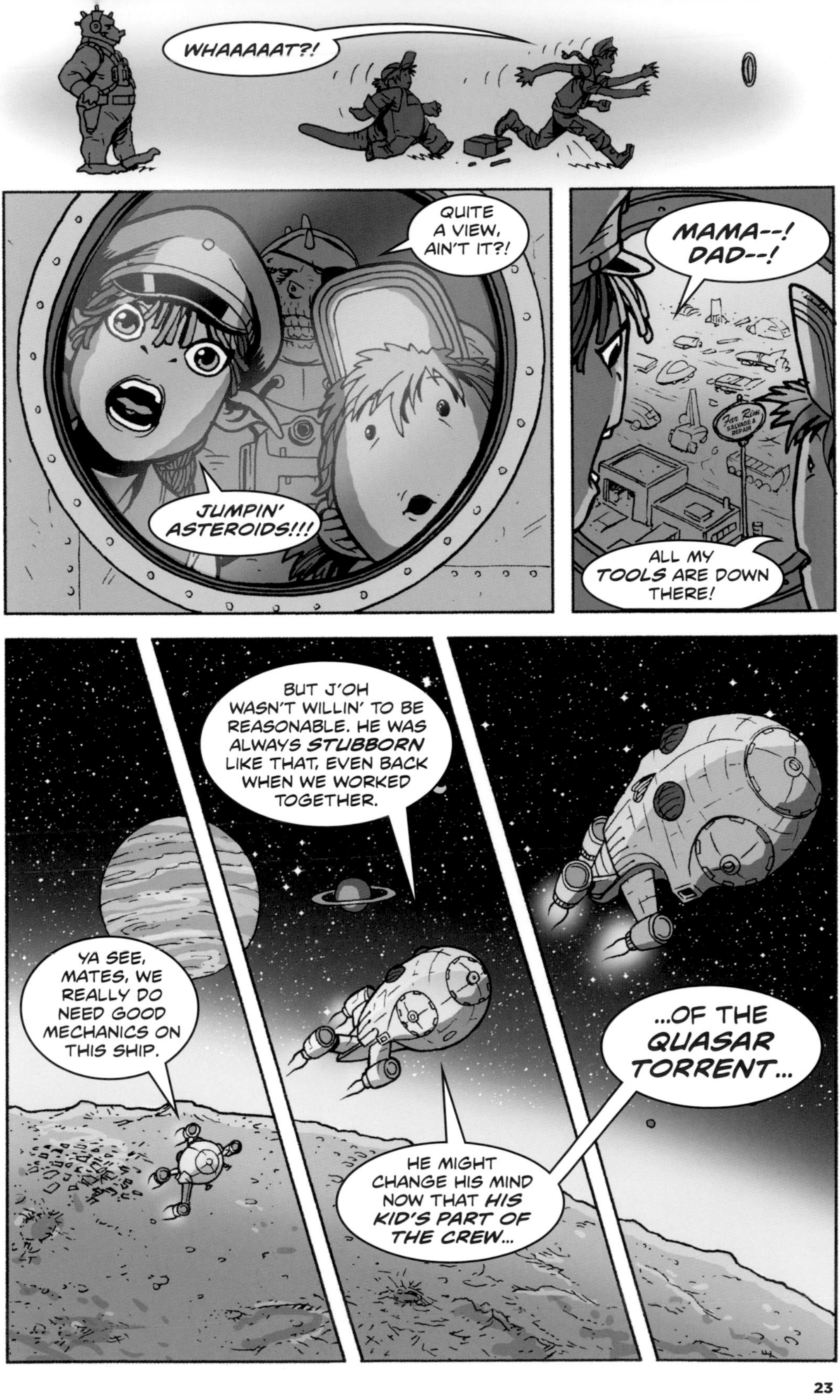

YA SEE, MATES, WE REALLY DO NEED GOOD MECHANICS ON THIS SHIP.

BUT J'OH WASN'T WILLIN' TO BE REASONABLE. HE WAS ALWAYS ***STUBBORN*** LIKE THAT, EVEN BACK WHEN WE WORKED TOGETHER.

HE MIGHT CHANGE HIS MIND NOW THAT *HIS KID'S PART OF THE CREW*...

...OF THE *QUASAR TORRENT*...

...THE FASTEST PIRATE SHIP ON THIS SIDE OF THE GALAXY!
REMEMBER HOW YOU ASKED WHAT'S THE WORST THAT COULD HAPPEN...?

I'M REALLY GONNA MISS THOSE TOOLS.

CHAPTER 2

IT'S BEEN THREE CYCLES! WHAT'S TAKIN' YOU TWO SO LONG?
I'M STARTIN' TO LOSE MY CONFIDENCE IN YA.

WELL, WE...UH...RAN INTO A COUPLE OF...ER... PROBLEMS...
...LIKE HAVING TO FIGURE OUT HOW THIS THING WORKS.

...BUT IT'S READY TO GO NOW! IT'LL WORK PERFECT!
WE HOPE.
'S GOOD THING...

CAN'T DO ANY REAL PIRATING WITHOUT A WORKIN' TRACTOR BEAM.
SO ZAM AND I HAVE HELD UP OUR PART OF THE DEAL-- YOUR BEAM IS *FIXED!*

SO NOW WE GET TO GO BACK HOME, RIGHT?
NOT 'TIL WE GET A-- LET'S CALL IT A *FINDER'S FEE*-- FROM YOUR PARENTS.

"FINDER'S FEE"? *HUH! RANSOM,* YOU MEAN!
H-HOW MUCH DID YOU ASK FOR US?

LET'S JUST SAY WE'RE STILL IN NEGOTIATIONS.
UM--KEEP IN MIND, THEY DON'T HAVE A *LOT* OF MONEY.

THIS IS THE BRIDGE, CAP'N. WE'VE GOT A CARGO SHIP SHOWIN' UP ON SENSORS!
PERFECT! I'LL BE RIGHT UP!
LOOKS LIKE WE GET TO PUT YOUR TRACTOR BEAM TO THE TEST, GIRLS. FOLLOW ME!
IT'LL WORK... RIGHT?
UM... PROBABLY.
QUARKCORP FREIGHTER DEAD AHEAD, CAP'N.
A QUARKCORP SHIP! GREAT!
LET'S LOCK ON TO 'ER! 5-4-3-2...
...1!
GOT IT!

WE'RE LOCKED ON TIGHT, CAP'N. STOPPED THE FREIGHTER RIGHT IN 'ER TRACKS.
WOW! I NEVER SEEN THE TRACTOR BEAM WORK THAT FAST BEFORE!

YOU GIRLS DONE GOOD!

SO WHAT'RE WE WAITING FOR? REEL 'ER IN AND TELL THE BOYS TO GET READY...

...TO LOOT 'ER AND THEN BLOW 'ER TO BITS!

Y-YOU *CAN'T!* YOU *WOULDN'T!*
HA! HA! WE DON'T CAPTURE FREIGHTERS SO'S WE CAN INVITE 'ER CREW OVER FOR TEA.

BEFORE LONG...
WE GOT 'ER ABOUT CLEANED OUT, CAP'N. LOOK'S LIKE WE GOT QUITE A HAUL!
THIRTY CRATES O' ENERGERIUM INGOTS! QUARKCORP WILL REALLY BE SQUEALING OVER THIS LOSS! HEH! HEH!
YOU'LL NEVER GET AWAY WITH THIS, YOU SPACE RATS!
QUARK CORP. FREIGHTER
1
YOU'RE THE SKIPPER O' THAT SCOW, ARE YA?
I AM! AND I'LL WARN YOU, ONCE QUARKCORP OFFICIALS HEAR ABOUT THIS OUTRAGE--
QUARK CORP.
HAR! WE'D LIKE TO SEE THE FACES ON THOSE CROOKS IN YOUR BOARDROOM WHEN THEY HEAR ABOUT THIS, WOULDN'T WE FELLAS?
SURE WOULD!
YOU BET!
SCOUNDRELS!

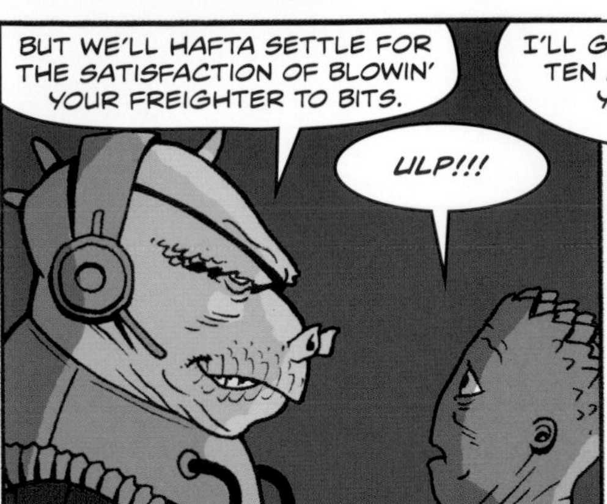
BUT WE'LL HAFTA SETTLE FOR THE SATISFACTION OF BLOWIN' YOUR FREIGHTER TO BITS.
ULP!!!

I'LL GIVE YOU AND YOUR CREW TEN MILLICYCLES TO GET IN YOUR LIFEPODS AND ABANDON SHIP...
...BEFORE THE THE WHOLE THING GOES
KA-BOOM!

...AND SAY HELLO TO YOUR BOSSES FROM THE CREW O' THE QUASAR TORRENT!
YAAAH!

YOU CAN'T J-J-JUST--?!
HEE!
HO! HO!

NAW. RELAX. AFTER ALL, WE AIN'T MONSTERS!
'COURSE NOT.
I JUST LIKE SEEIN' THEIR REACTION WHEN I TELL 'EM THAT.

PLUS, BY THE TIME THEY REALIZE IT WAS A BLUFF, WE'LL BE LONG GONE!
GIVES US A HEAD START ON ANY LOCAL LAW THEY MIGHT CALL.
NOW LET'S DO SOME CELEBRATIN'! *TO THE GALLEY, BOYS!*

MOMENTS LATER...
SO THIS IS A *PARTY?!* I'VE NEVER BEEN TO ONE BEFORE.
ME NEITHER.

HEY, FELLAS--HOW 'BOUT A CHEER FOR OUR NEW *TRACTOR BEAM GENIUSES!*
YEAH!

RAH!
RAH!
RAH!

NICE WORK, GIRLIE. WHERE'D YOU LEARN TO TEAR DOWN SOMETHIN' AS COMPLICATED AS A TRACTOR BEAM?
HA! I WAS RAISED WITH A WRENCH IN MY HAND.
...AND IT TURNS OUT THIS RIG WORKS ON THE SAME PRINCIPLE AS AN OLD BEAM GENERATOR WE TINKERED WITH ONCE, SO...

HEY--*HOLOCARDS!* WHAT GAME ARE YOU GUYS PLAYIN'?
DEAD MAN'S FLUSH. KNOW HOW?

SURE! I BEAT THE 'BOTS BACK HOME AT THIS ALL THE TIME!
LET 'ER PLAY, STACHE. LET'S SEE WHAT SHE CAN DO!

YOU FELLAS KNOW HOW TO PLAY CIRILLIAN RULES?

ASTROJACKS ARE WILD, AND NO DRAWING FROM THE GRID UNLESS YOU ANTE UP!
AND REMEMBER-- IT'S ONLY CALLED "CHEATING" IF THEY *CATCH YOU* AT IT!

...SO WE FIGURED IF WE REBUILT THE COIL CHARGERS...
HA! OUR OLD MECHANIC WOULDA NEVER THOUGHT O' THAT, EH, FYNN?
ABSOLUTELY!

OOOHH! A ROBOT ARM! COOL!
AWW-- KEEPS SHORTIN' OUT ON ME, THOUGH.

YOUR SERVO MOTORS JUST NEED A LITTLE ADJUSTMENT, I BET.
LEMME TAKE A LOOK.

TRY IT NOW.
HUH. YEAH. THAT FEELS BETTER.

YOU'RE ALL RIGHT, KID!
HEY, THE DONUT PRINTER'S BEEN ACTIN' UP. CAN YA TAKE A LOOK AT IT?
UH... WELL, SURE. I GUESS.

WHAT'S YOUR MOVE, KID?
DON'T RUSH ME.

IT DON'T PUT ON ENOUGH SPRINKLES NO MORE.
HMMM.

I'LL SEE YOUR TEN CREDITS AND RAISE YOU FIFTEEN MORE.
HA! SHE'S GOT GUTS!

THESE JETS ARE ALL CLOGGED.

YOU'LL HAVE TO CHEAT BETTER THAN THAT, MISTER.
HAR! SHARP EYES ON THIS ONE!

YUM! GOOD AS NEW!
LEMME TWEAK IT A BIT MORE.

FULL SPAN--NEUTRONS HIGH!
GASP!

NOW *THAT'S* A SPRINKLED DONUT.

GAH! I FIGURED YOU WAS BLUFFIN'!
WIN!

WE PROWL THE SPACEWAYS, HI-HIDY-YO! WE ROAM FROM STAR TO STAR--
WE WANDER THROUGH THE INKY BLACK IN SEARCH OF TREASURE NEAR AND FAR!
HIDY-HIDY-YO-YO-YO!
HIDY-HIDY-YO!
LOOKS LIKE THE NEW CREW MEMBERS ARE GONNA FIT RIGHT IN, CAP'N.
WHO ASKED YA? TURNS OUT THEY ACTUALLY ARE PRETTY GOOD MECHANICS, THOUGH.
THAT MIGHT SIMPLIFY MY PLANS A LITTLE.

LATER...
RISE AND SHINE, YOU TWO!
UGH! UH--RED MYK? WH-WHAT--?!

OHHH. MY TONGUE TASTES TERRIBLE.

I MIGHTA HAD A FEW TOO MANY OF THOSE SPRINKLY DONUTS, MYSELF.

TIME FOR YOU LADIES TO GET TO WORK.
BUT THE TRACTOR BEAM'S FIXED.
YOU THINK THAT WAS THE ONLY THING NEEDS FIXIN' ON THIS SHIP? HA!

YOU NEED TO TUNE UP THE BOOSTERS ON ENGINE THREE TODAY.
WE'RE NOT YOUR SLAVES, YOU KNOW! SO JUST--
CLICK
GRRR!!!
BOOSTER TUNE-UP, HUH. LET'S GO TAKE A LOOK.

SO WE'RE JUST GONNA DO WHATEVER WE'RE TOLD?!
DO WE HAVE A CHOICE?

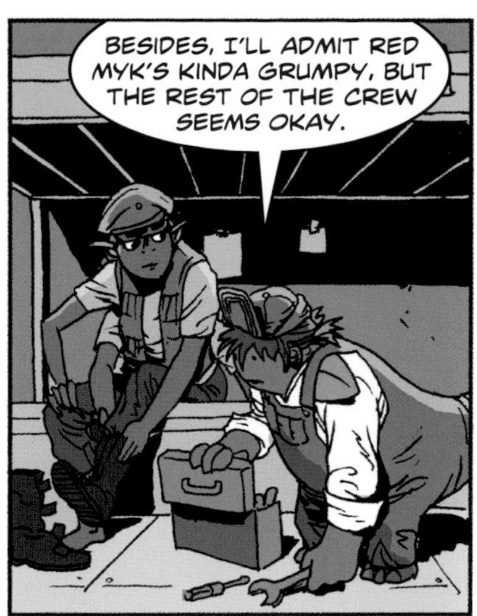
BESIDES, I'LL ADMIT RED MYK'S KINDA GRUMPY, BUT THE REST OF THE CREW SEEMS OKAY.

A FEW SPRINKLY DONUTS IS ALL IT TAKES TO WIN YOU OVER, EH?
THOSE WERE GOOD.
AREN'T YOU WORRIED ABOUT WHEN WE'LL GET BACK HOME?

HOME--? HMM...
I LIKED YOUR FAMILY'S SCRAPYARD...
...BUT LOOK AT ALL THE COOL STUFF WE'VE GOT TO WORK WITH ON THIS SHIP! WHAT MORE COULD YOU WANT?

I WANNA GO HOME!

AW, I'M SURE WE'LL BE BACK HOME SOON...
...BUT UNTIL THEN, WE MAY AS WELL TAKE ADVANTAGE OF HAVIN' THIS BIG TOY TO WORK ON.

THINK WE CAN GET THE CARBON SCORING OFF'A THESE CONTACTS?
MAYBE. LET'S TRY THE ULTRASONIC CHISEL.
IF YOU RE-SOLDER THOSE CIRCUIT BOARDS...
...IT SHOULD SOLVE THE SHORT-CIRCUITS IN THE FUEL DISTRIBUTORS.
YEP! THE LITHIUM CORE IN HERE IS CRACKED, ALL RIGHT. I CAN ALMOST REACH IT!
CHECK THE ION CELLS, TOO, WHILE YOU'RE IN THERE.
I BET WE COULD INCREASE THE POWER ON THESE IF WE RE-JIGGERED THE CIRCUITS A BIT.
'S WORTH A TRY.

OOPS! GUESS I FORGOT TO WARN YOU I WAS GONNA START THOSE GEARS.
REALLY.
FYNN, YOU GOTTA KEEP YOUR--ER--PET OUTTA THE DUCTS! THEY'RE SCREWIN' UP THE OXYGEN SENSORS.
SQUIGGY!
WHEW! AT THE RATE WE'RE GOING, WE MIGHT RUN OUT OF STUFF TO FIX ON THIS TUB PRETTY SOON.
NOT LIKELY. THIS OLD SHIP NEEDS MORE WORK THAN THE TWO OF US WILL EVER GET TO.
YOU BOTH LOOK BEAT. COME TAKE A BREAK.
YEAH. SNACKS ARE ON US.

...AND MY LASER'S WORKING PERFECT SINCE YOU FIXED IT.
SPYK JUST MADE SOME BROWNIES. WANT ONE?
YA KNOW, YOU GUYS SURE SEEM NICE FOR--YOU KNOW--*PIRATES.*
YEAH! I THOUGHT PIRATES WERE SUPPOSED TO BE GRUFF AND MEAN.

WE AIN'T *GRUFF?!*
FACT IS, WE'RE PRETTY NEW TO THIS PIRATE STUFF.
WELL, YOU'RE *SORTA* GRUFF--

I *USED* TO BE A SPACE TRUCKER.
I WORKED AT A NUCLEAR FILLIN' STATION RIGHT ALONG THE OLD SPACEPIKE.
I RAN A DINER ON GLAXON 5.
WE *ALL* HAD LEGIT JOBS BEFORE THIS.
SO HOW'D YOU GUYS END UP AS PIRATES?
WELL, LEMME TELL YA...

EVEN THOUGH THIS SPACE SECTOR IS WAY OUT ON THE EDGE OF THE GALAXY, WE STILL FOUND PLENTY OF WAYS TO MAKE A LIVIN'.
YOU ARE HERE.
USED TO BE THAT THE *FAR RIM* SECTOR WAS CRAWLIN' WITH SHIPS AND SHUTTLES PASSIN' THROUGH TO GET FROM ANDROMEDA TO THE CENTER OF THE GALAXY--
LOTS OF FUEL STATIONS, RESTAURANTS, SATELLITES, TOW SHIPS-- STUFF LIKE THAT. WE ALL MADE DECENT LIVINGS OFF FAR RIM'S TRAFFIC.
QUARKCORP
QUARKCORP
THAT ALL CHANGED WHEN *QUARKCORP*, A BIG-TIME SPACE-FREIGHT COMPANY, DISCOVERED A WORMHOLE OUT ON THE EDGE OF QUADRANT 47.

TURNED OUT THE WORMHOLE WAS A SHORTCUT THROUGH SPACE! SHIPS COULD PASS THROUGH IT...
...SKIPPIN' RIGHT BY FAR RIM...
...TO GET STRAIGHT TO THE BUSY CENTER OF THE GALAXY!
QUARKCORP SET UP A TOLLGATE AROUND THE WORMHOLE--EVEN NAMED IT QUARK'S GATE.

THEY ENDED UP CONTROLLIN' ALL THE SECTOR'S TRAFFIC-- EVERY SHIP PASSIN' THROUGH EITHER BELONGED TO THEIR FLEET OR PAID THEM A TOLL.
WE WAS ALL OUTTA WORK BEFORE TOO LONG!
JEEZ.
AFTER THAT, SHIPS NEVER STOPPED IN FAR RIM--THEY JUST PASSED RIGHT BY. ALL THE BUSINESSES DRIED UP! THE WHOLE AREA BECAME A GHOST SECTOR!

THAT'S WHEN RED MYK HAD THE IDEA TO START PIRATIN'. WE JOINED UP ON THE *QUASAR TORRENT* TO RAID QUARKCORP'S FREIGHTERS ON THEIR WAY TO THE WORMHOLE.
THEY *RUINED OUR LIVES*, SO WE DECIDED TO *RUIN THEIRS!*

SO THAT'S WHY *FAR RIM* IS SUCH A LONESOME SPOT IN SPACE! HEY ROX, I BET THAT'S HOW J'OH AND YOUR MOM ENDED UP ON THAT ASTEROID!
MAYBE. MOM SAID THEY BOTH WORKED ON A SPACE STATION NEAR SIRIUS BACK WHEN I WAS FIRST BORN.

J'OH--FROM STATION SIRIUS?! HEY, IS YOUR DAD *J'OH ALDEBARAN?*
UM-- YEAH.
I HEARD OF HIM-- THAT GUY WAS THE BEST QUANTUM MECHANIC IN THE FAR RIM SECTOR!

IN THE OLD DAYS, MYK WAS A PILOT ON A LITTLE FREIGHTER LINE. J'OH WAS HIS MECHANIC.
BUT MYK AND J'OH HAD SOME KIND OF FALLIN' OUT. I HEARD J'OH FINALLY REFUSED TO DO ANY MORE WORK FOR HIM.

ER--WELL, ZAM--WE'D BETTER GET BACK TO WORK.
YEAH. WE'VE STILL GOTTA CHECK ON THOSE POWER CELL FAILURES ON THE LOWER DECK.
THANKS FOR THE BROWNIES, FELLAS.

NICE BUNCHA GUYS.
THEY *ARE* NICE. BUT STILL--THEY *DID* KIDNAP US!

I WISH I KNEW WHAT'S TAKING MOM AND DAD SO LONG TO PAY OUR RANSOM.
I'M WORRIED THEY DON'T HAVE THE MONEY.

WELL, IF OUR *SIDE PROJECT* WORKS OUT, MAYBE THEY WON'T NEED TO PAY UP.
SHH!!! NOT SO LOUD!
OOPS! RIGHT.

ANYWAY, LET'S SEE IF WE CAN FIGURE OUT WHAT'S UP WITH THOSE BAD POWER CELLS.

CHAPTER 3

CREW STAY OUT!!
ROX AND ZAM'S PLACE
GIRLS NEED PRIVACY!
PSST! ZAM!
DID YA GET IT?

I TOOK IT OUT OF THE BACK-UP ARRAY WHILE I WAS FIXING AXYL'S CONSOLE UP ON THE BRIDGE.

THEY SHOULDN'T MISS IT.

LET'S HOOK IT UP TO THE "LIFEBOAT."

ONCE WE GET A NAVIGATION SYSTEM WORKING ON THIS THING...

...WE'LL HOP IN, SLIP OUT THE SHIP'S WASTE-EJECTION PORT, THEN HEAD FOR HOME.

IT'S NOT *THAT* SIMPLE, ROX.

THIS THING'S A JUMBLE OF PARTS SWIPED FROM ALL OVER THE SHIP. I HOPE EVERYTHING WORKS OKAY TOGETHER.
SHE'LL BE FINE! YOU GOTTA HAVE CONFIDENCE, ZAM!

WE'RE LUCKY WE FOUND THE TIME TO BUILD THIS THING, WHAT WITH RED MYK'S MAINTENANCE ORDERS, PLUS THE REQUESTS WE'VE BEEN GETTING FROM THE CREW.
SEE IF YOU CAN HOOK UP THAT NAV BOARD. I PROMISED SPYK I'D LOOK AT HIS DISINTEGRATOR.

I KINDA MISS YOU LATELY, ZAM. ONE OF US IS ALWAYS IN HERE WORKING ON THE ESCAPE POD WHILE THE OTHER IS OUT REPAIRING SOMETHING ON THE SHIP.
IT'S NICE THE CREW'S BEEN SO FRIENDLY, THOUGH.

I DECIDED YOU'RE RIGHT--THEY DO SEEM LIKE A NICE BUNCH.
THE ONLY ONE THAT TREATS US LIKE WE'RE *PRISONERS* IS RED MYK.

HE'S NOT JUST GROUCHY TO US--HE YELLS AT THE CREW A LOT, TOO.
THE ONLY THING THEY LIKE *LESS* THAN MYK IS *QUARK-CORP!*

AND Y'KNOW, I DON'T BLAME 'EM! THAT COMPANY RUINED THE LIVES OF EVERYONE IN *FAR RIM*--MY FAMILY INCLUDED! AND THEY CALL *US* PIRATES!

"US"? YOU MEAN THE CREW.
BUT *WE* AIN'T *PIRATES*, ROX.
WE'RE ALL IN THE SAME SITUATION, ZAM.
AHH! HERE'S THE PROBLEM.

'COURSE NOT. I'M JUST SAYING I UNDERSTAND HOW THEY FEEL.
THAT OUGHT TO DO IT.

ZAP!

FIXED!

I'M GONNA KINDA MISS THE QUASAR TORRENT ONCE WE ESCAPE.
IT IS A COOL SHIP.

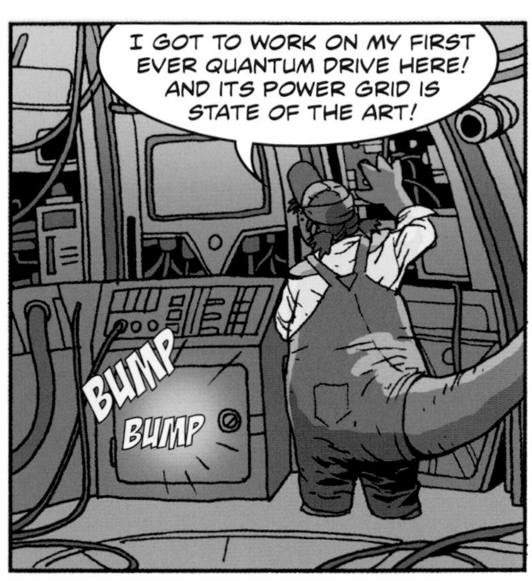
I GOT TO WORK ON MY FIRST EVER QUANTUM DRIVE HERE! AND ITS POWER GRID IS STATE OF THE ART!
BUMP
BUMP

STATE OF THE ART?! THEN WHY ARE WE ALWAYS REPLACING POWER CELLS ALL OVER THE SHIP?
UM...WELL... THAT MIGHT BE FROM NORMAL WEAR AND TEAR.

DOESN'T SEEM NORMAL TO ME.

THERE'S SOMETHING WEIRD GOING ON WITH THOSE CELLS!
OH, WELL...
SLAM!

...I GUESS A SHIP THIS BIG IS BOUND TO HAVE A FEW MYSTERIES!

I'M GONNA RETURN THIS DISINTEGRATOR TO SPYK. C'MON ALONG! I HEARD THERE WAS CAKE IN THE GALLEY.
NAW. I BETTER KEEP WORKIN'.
YOU CAN TAKE A BREAK, ZAM. HEY, MAYBE WE CAN GET IN ON A HOLOCARD GAME WITH SOME OF THE GUYS!
YOU GO AHEAD. I WANNA PRESSURIZE THE POD AND TEST FOR AIR LEAKS.
WELL...OKAY.
I'LL SEE YOU LATER, ZAM.
YEAH, LATER.

...AND THAT'S WHY YOU NEVER TELL A BORALLIAN TO WATCH YOUR LUNCH WHILE YOU USE THE BATHROOM!
HAR! HAR!
HA! THAT'S A GOOD ONE, KID!

WHAT'RE *YOU* DOIN' IN HERE, GIRLIE?!
TAKE IT EASY, MYK. SHE WAS JUST...

SHE AIN'T HERE TO "JUST" ANYTHING! NOT WHEN WE GOT POWER CELLS FAILIN' LEFT AND RIGHT ON THIS SHIP!

THAT AIN'T HER FAULT, MYK. IT'S THOSE *GREMLINS! SPACE GREMLINS!*
SPACE GREMLINS?!
PATCH, THAT'S NOT A REAL THING.

AS REAL AS YOU AND ME! I *SEEN* ONE DOWN ON DECK THREE!
RILLY?!
WELL--DROPPIN'S FROM ONE, AND RIGHT NEAR A CHEWED-UP POWER CABLE! *HAD* TO BE GREMLINS, I TELL YA!

ALL I KNOW IS, THOSE POWER CELLS NEED FIXIN'. GET TO WORK!
ALL RIGHT. ALL RIGHT.

JEEZ, MYK! SHE WAS ONLY TAKIN' A QUICK BREAK WITH US.

I DON'T LIKE YOU BUMS TREATIN' HER AND HER PAL LIKE THEY'RE *MASCOTS* OR SOMETHIN'!
THOSE GIRLS ARE HERE TO DO A JOB, *AND I'M GONNA MAKE 'EM DO IT!*

HEY, ROX! HOW'S IT GOIN'?
WELL, ROB...IT WAS GOIN' FINE UP UNTIL RED MYK SHOWED UP!

WHOOOOOP! WHOOOOOP!
JEEZ, GIL-- WHAT'S THAT?!
RED ALERT!!! WE'RE UNDER ATTACK!

BATTLE STATIONS-- ON THE DOUBLE!
WHOOOOOP!
ZAM! ZAM!
WHAT'S GOIN' ON, AXYL-- REPORT!
WE GOT A QUARKCORP SHIP --INTRUDER CLASS-- COMIN' UP ON US FAST, CAP'N!
I'M PICKIN' UP A MESSAGE FROM THEM, TOO!
THIS IS THE COMMANDER OF THE NEUTRON STORM HAILING THE QUASAR TORRENT. SURRENDER OR WE BLOW YOU FROM THE SKY.

SWITCH ALL POWER TO THE QUANTUM DRIVES--WE'LL TRY AND OUTRUN IT!
UH...CAP'N, WE'VE GOT POWER SHORTFALLS IN TWO ENGINES!
@#!&!!!
ENGINE ROOM-- YOU'VE GOT TWO MILLICYCLES TO GET US OUT OF HERE...
...OR WE GET BLOWN TO BITS!!!
ZAP! ZAP!
ZAP! ZAP!
ZAM! WHAT'RE YOU DOIN'?!
THE REGULATORS CAN'T DIRECT ENOUGH JUICE INTO THE SYSTEM TO FORCE THE ENGINES TO FULL CAPACITY...
...BECAUSE OF THOSE POWER CELL FAILURES!
ENGINE ROOM, REPORT!!!
RED MYK'S NOT GONNA LIKE THAT ANSWER!

ZA-POW!

WE'RE *HIT!* ENGINE TWO IS OFFLINE!

ENGINE 2: NEGATIV

EVASIVE MANEUVERS! KEEP US OUTTA THOSE PHOTON BEAMS!

YOU GIRLS BETTER THINK *FAST*...

...'CAUSE WE GOTTA OUTRUN THAT SHIP OR WE'RE ***TOAST!***

...SO MAYBE IF WE REROUTE POWER LINES...

LET'S TRY THE TRACTOR BEAM!
?!?!

WE'RE TRYIN' TO ESCAPE FROM THOSE GUYS, NOT PULL 'EM IN CLOSER!
WELL, YEAH...

...BUT IF WE REARRANGE SOME CONNECTIONS AND REVERSE POLARITY ON THE COILS...

...WE GET A REPELLER BEAM--MAYBE! LET'S TRY IT!!!

YOU RE-JIGGER THE CONNECTIONS! I'LL REPROGRAM THE SYSTEM!
I'M ON IT!

WE CAN'T KEEP OUTTA THEIR FIRE FOREVER, CAP'N!
MAYBE WE SHOULD THINK ABOUT--
SURRENDER?! NOT A CHANCE!

AND WE'RE NOT GOIN' DOWN WITHOUT A FIGHT! TURN THIS SHIP ABOUT!

WE'RE GONNA ATTACK AN INTRUDER CLASS SHIP?!
WE'RE DOOMED.

I'M READY OVER HERE, ZAM!
I'M SET, TOO! LIGHT 'ER UP!

HERE WE GO!

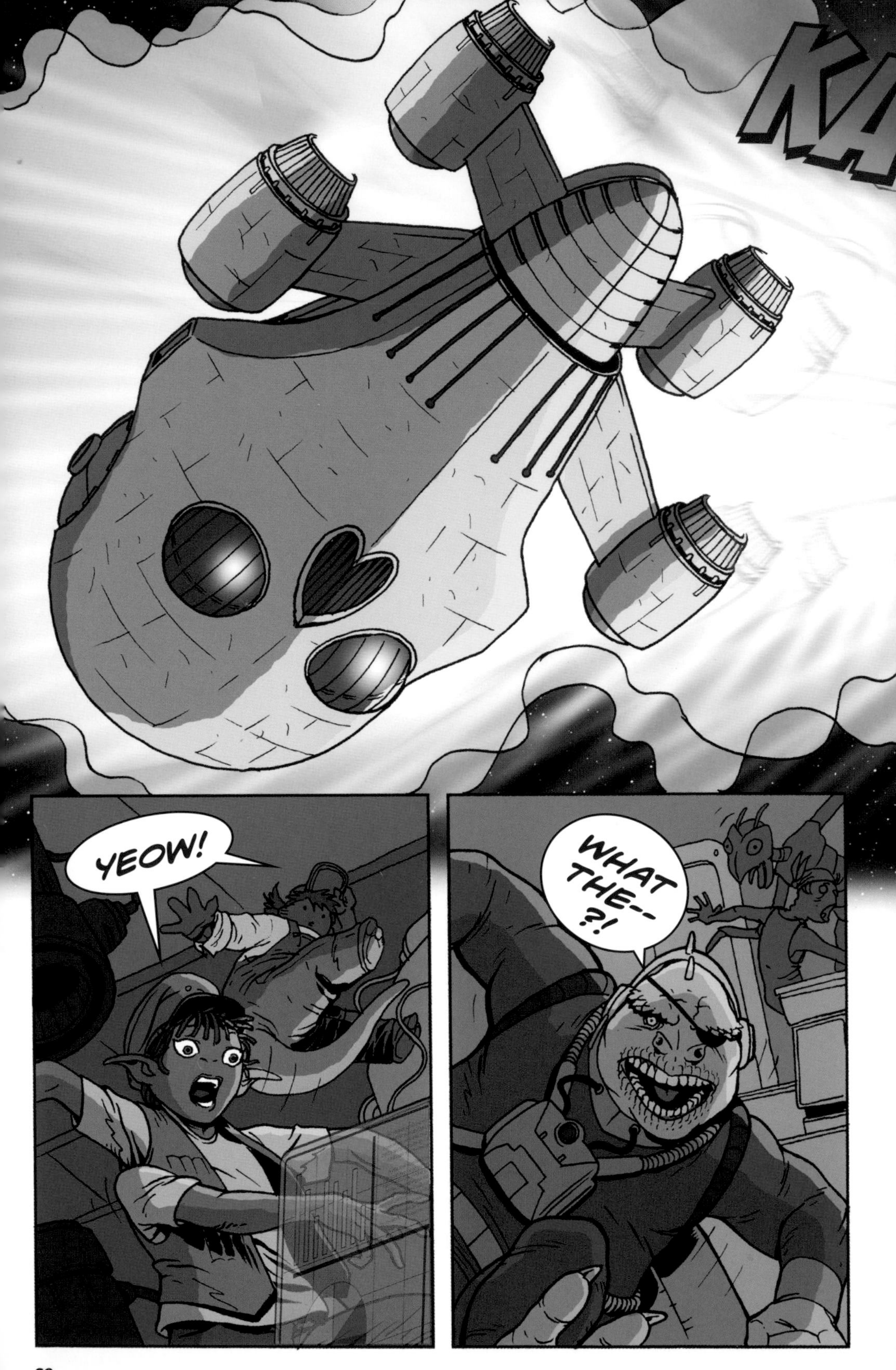
KA
YEOW!
WHAT THE-- ?!

BOING!
WE'VE LEAPED AHEAD OF 'EM, CAP'N! NOW WE'VE GOT A GOOD HEAD START!
THEN LET'S GET OUT OF HERE!

WE MADE IT! THEY'RE TOO BIG TO FOLLOW US INTO THIS ASTEROID FIELD! THEY'LL *NEVER* CATCH US NOW!

DON'T KNOW WHAT THOSE GIRLS DID, BUT THEY SURE *SAVED OUR SKINS!*

THOSE TWO ARE THE BEST MECHANICS THIS SHIP'S EVER HAD!

--A PAIR OF *GENIUSES!*

YOU'RE THE ONE WHO SAID BAD POWER CELLS WERE THE CAUSE OF THE TROUBLE.
I'M...AH... NOT REALLY POSITIVE. COULD BE SOMETHIN' ELSE, LIKE FAULTY--

C'MON! YOU KNOW IT'S THE POWER CELLS!
GRAB YOUR TOOLS. LET'S GO CHECK OUT THE CELLS BY ENGINE TWO.
UM--

YOU GO ON AHEAD. I GOTTA DO A--YOU KNOW-- A THING BEFORE I CAN...
WELL... OKAY, I GUESS.

SINCE WHEN DOESN'T THAT GIRL WANT TO GO CRAWLIN' AROUND IN A QUANTUM DRIVE?
WEIRD!

I WONDER HOW MUCH DAMAGE THAT PHOTON HIT DID TO THIS ENGINE.

IT'S KINDA CREEPY IN HERE.

?!? WHAT'S THIS?

LOOKS LIKE SOME KIND OF TRACKS... AND...
...*ANIMAL DROPPINGS!*
GROSS!

THERE'S A POWER CELL.
ALMOST LOOKS LIKE...

...SOME-THING'S BEEN *CHEWING* ON IT?!

THIS WHOLE ARRAY OF CELLS IS--
RUSTLE

RUSTLE
SQUEAK
RUSTLE
?!?

YIKES!

...SPACE GREMLIN!!!

HOLD STILL!
BOING!
BOING!

YOU'RE WAY TOO FAST! OKAY, LET'S TRY THIS A DIFFERENT WAY.
YOU LIKE POWER CELLS, DO YOU?

HOW WOULD YOU LIKE A DELICIOUS, FULLY CHARGED...

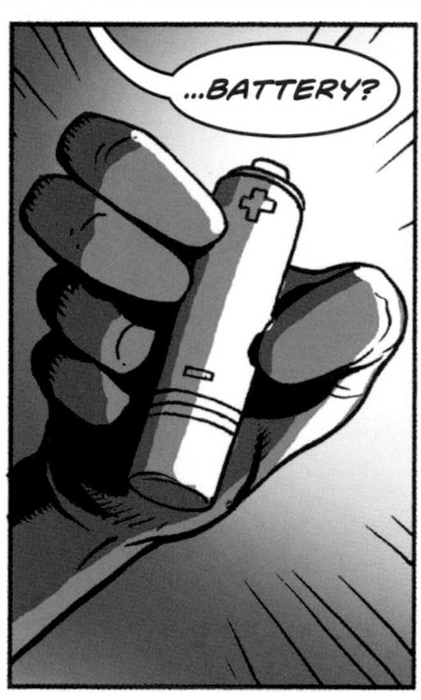
...BATTERY?

THAT'S RIGHT--IT'S ALL YOURS! JUST COME A *LITTLE* CLOSER...

GOTCHA!
GLEEP?!?

ZAM! ZAM! I GOT ONE!
"GOT ONE"? ONE OF WHAT?

A SPACE GREMLIN!
HE PUT UP QUITE A FIGHT, TOO!
PATCH TOLD ME ABOUT 'EM. I DIDN'T BELIEVE HIM...

...BUT LOOK!

THIS LITTLE GUY'S BEEN CHEWIN' UP ALL THE POWER CELLS! HE--

GLEEP!

SPROING!

BAD, TILDA! BAD!

SIGH. C'MON, ROX...

I GUESS IT'S TIME TO FILL YOU IN.

OKAY, SO DON'T FREAK OUT ON ME...
...BUT I'VE BEEN KEEPING A SECRET FOR THE LAST BUNCHA CYCLES.

REALLY-- DON'T FREAK OUT.

CHAPTER 4

SO...UM...
...TURNS OUT WE'RE NOT THE ONLY ACCIDENTAL TRAVELERS ON BOARD THE *QUASAR TORRENT*.

WHAT ARE THESE THINGS?!
THEY'RE BABY ZOLORIANS.
ZOLORIANS?!? THEY'RE LIKE YOU?!?
WELL... THEY'RE FROM MY HOME PLANET, ANYWAY.
HOW--? WHERE DID--? WHEN--?
I CAME ACROSS TILDA HOLED UP IN THE POWER ROUTER WHILE WE WERE WORKIN' ON ENGINE FOUR A WHILE BACK.
SHE LED ME TO THE OTHERS.
THEY'D BEEN CHEWIN' ON THE POWER CELLS ALL OVER THE SHIP --THE LITTLE STINKERS-- SO I BROUGHT 'EM BACK HERE TO KEEP 'EM OUT OF TROUBLE.

WHERE'D THEY *COME FROM?!*

WELL, I CAN'T SAY FOR SURE. THEY'RE TOO YOUNG TO TALK...

...BUT I'VE GOT A PRETTY GOOD *GUESS.*

ROX, DID YOU EVER WONDER HOW I ENDED UP ON YOUR PARENTS' ASTEROID?

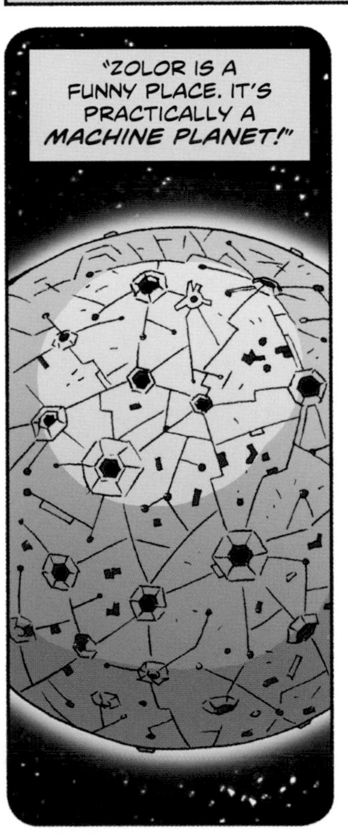

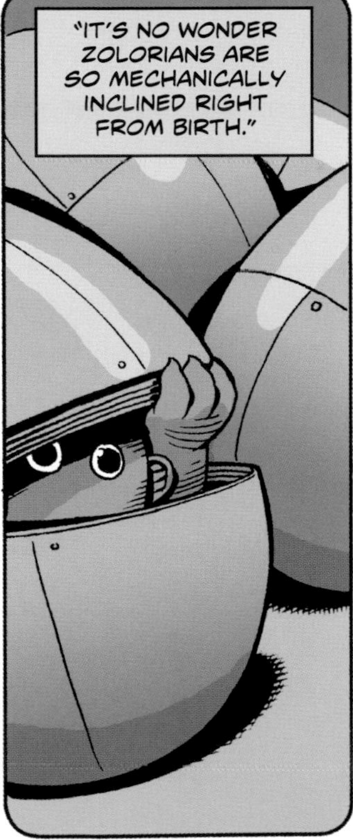

"ZOLORIANS DON'T REALLY DO THE PARENTING THING. WE *TAKE CARE OF OURSELVES* RIGHT FROM BIRTH..."

"...AND WE'RE BORN WITH A REAL FASCINATION FOR *GADGETS*-- WE CAN'T STAY AWAY FROM ANYTHING MECHANICAL!"

"ONE DAY WHEN AN OLD TRADING SHIP SET DOWN NEAR MY HOME, I JUST COULDN'T RESIST..."

"...TAKIN' A CLOSER LOOK."

"THAT SHIP REALLY HAD SOME DELICIOUS POWER SUPPLIES!"
"YOU *EAT* POWER SUPPLIES?!?"
"*OF COURSE!* ZOLORIANS *LIVE* ON THOSE! *MMMM*...NICKEL-METAL HYDRIDE, AND LITHIUM CELLS! *YUM!*
"THOUGH LATELY I'VE STARTED LIKIN' *BROWNIES*, TOO."

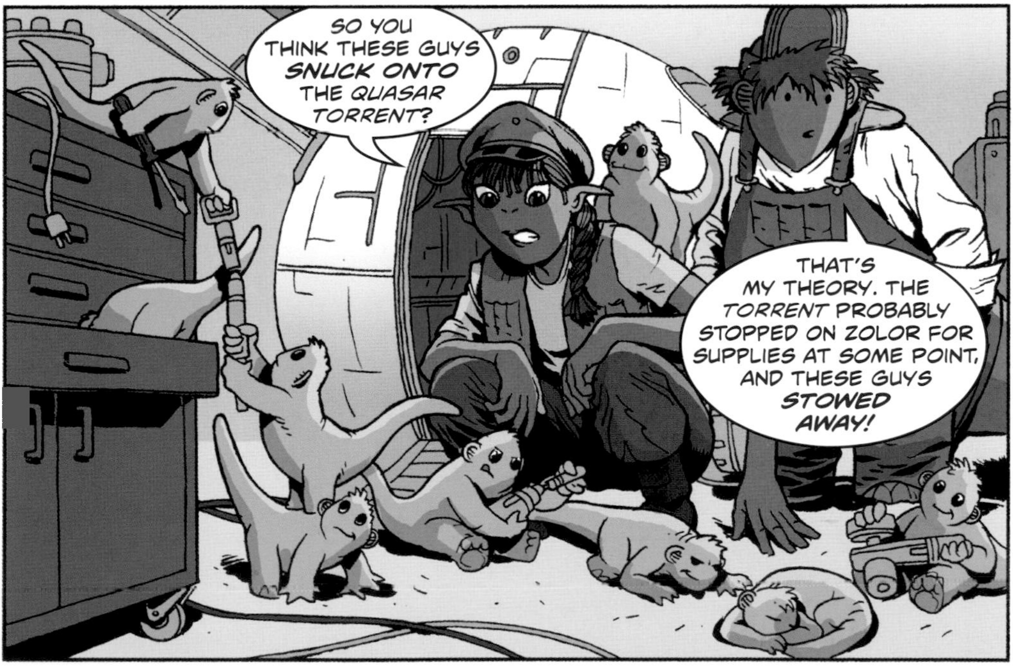

SO YOU THINK THESE GUYS ***SNUCK ONTO*** THE *QUASAR TORRENT*?

THAT'S MY THEORY. THE *TORRENT* PROBABLY STOPPED ON ZOLOR FOR SUPPLIES AT SOME POINT, AND THESE GUYS ***STOWED AWAY!***

WHY DIDN'T YOU TELL ME ABOUT 'EM?!
THE CREW THINKS THEY'RE GREMLINS-- SOME KINDA PESTS! AND YOU'VE BEEN HANGIN' WITH THOSE GUYS SO MUCH LATELY I WAS AFRAID YOU MIGHT AGREE WITH 'EM.

I THOUGHT IF I COULD ROUND THEM ALL UP AND FEED THEM ON WORN OUT BATTERY PACKS, THEY'D STOP WRECKIN' THINGS.
'CEPT TILDA KEEPS ESCAPING TO GO SNACK ON ENGINE TWO!

HEY!!!
ACTUALLY, I'VE BEEN TRAINING THEM TO HELP OUT ON THE SHIP.
THEY CAN GET INTO SMALL SPACES YOU AND I CAN'T REACH.

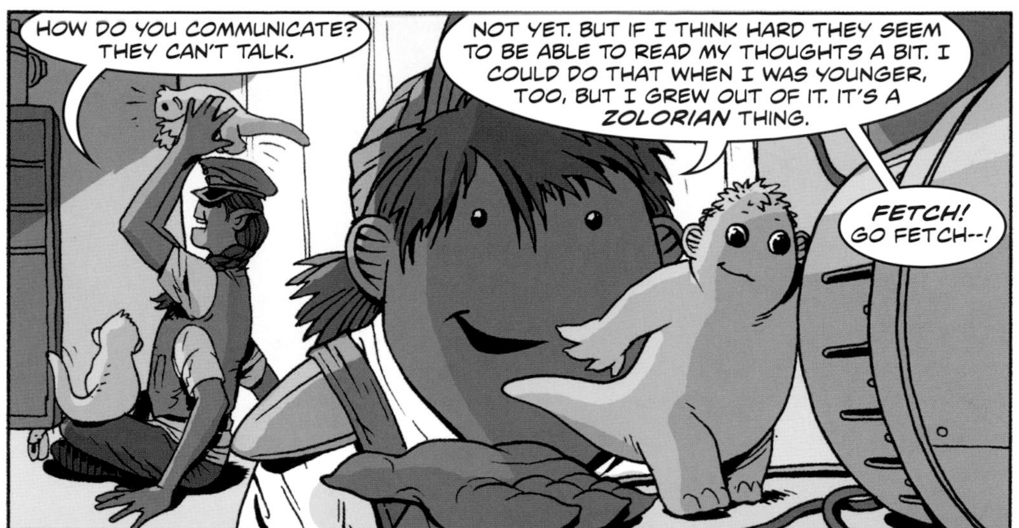
HOW DO YOU COMMUNICATE? THEY CAN'T TALK.
NOT YET. BUT IF I THINK HARD THEY SEEM TO BE ABLE TO READ MY THOUGHTS A BIT. I COULD DO THAT WHEN I WAS YOUNGER, TOO, BUT I GREW OUT OF IT. IT'S A ZOLORIAN THING.
FETCH! GO FETCH--!

YOU MIGHT BE RIGHT ABOUT THE CREW. I'M NOT SURE THEY'D BE COOL WITH THESE GUYS AFTER ALL THE TROUBLE THEY CAUSED.
LOOK FOR THE BROKEN RESISTOR!
MEEP!
YOU CAN DO IT!

YOU CAN TRUST ME, ZAM! I WON'T TELL!
MEEP!
GOOD GIRL, TILDA!

BUT WE HAVE TO MAKE SURE NONE OF THESE GUYS ESCAPE AGAIN.
YEAH. TILDA IS BAD ABOUT THA--

KNOCK! KNOCK!
GAAAH!

HEY, GIRLS-- I BEEN HAVING TROUBLE WITH MY ELECTRIC TOOTH...

...BRUSH.

PATCH! YOU KNOW BETTER THAN TO COME IN HERE!
"CREW-- STAY OUT!" THE SIGN SAYS!
SORRY-- UM--BUT SEE-- MY TOOTHBRUSH IS--
ARE YOU TWO ALL RIGHT?

WE'RE FINE! SET YOUR TOOTHBRUSH OVER THERE. WE'LL TAKE A LOOK AT IT...
...AS LONG AS YOU PROMISE NOT TO JUST STROLL INTO OUR *PRIVATE QUARTERS* ANYMORE!

SORRY, ROX. SORRY, ZAM.
JUS' LEMME KNOW ABOUT THE TOOTHBRUSH WHEN YOU CAN.
DO YOU THINK HE--?

NAH. IT'S A GOOD THING PATCH ISN'T THE SHARPEST TOOL IN THE TOOLBOX.
STILL, THAT WAS *CLOSE!*

KEEPIN' THESE GUYS A *SECRET* MAY GET KINDA *TRICKY!*
SHOO! SHOO, EVERYBODY! BACK INTO YOUR *BOX!*

ALL HANDS REPORT TO THE GALLEY *IMMEDIATELY! MOVE IT, YOU BUMS!*
RED MYK!

DO YOU THINK HE *KNOWS?!*
SOUNDS LIKE WE'RE ABOUT TO FIND OUT.

THIS SHIP'S MISSION IS TO *STICK IT TO QUARKCORP* IN ANY WAY POSSIBLE. BUT WE CAN'T DO THAT HIDIN' IN THE MIDDLE OF AN ASTEROID FIELD!
WE NEED TO *ELIMINATE* THE SOURCE OF THESE POWER FAILURES...
HERE IT COMES!
...AND I EXPECT *YOU TWO* TO SOLVE THE PROBLEM *FAST, OR ELSE--!*

SO...YOU *DON'T KNOW* WHAT THE PROBLEM *IS?*
NO WORRIES, MYK. WE'VE ALREADY GOT IT ALL FIGURED OUT. THERE'LL BE NO MORE POWER FAILURES FROM NOW ON!

EVEN WITH FULL POWER, WE DON'T STAND A CHANCE AGAINST THAT INTRUDER-CLASS SHIP IN A FAIR FIGHT!
AND THEY'RE SURE TO BE READY FOR THAT REVERSED TRACTOR BEAM TRICK THE NEXT TIME WE SEE 'EM!
IF ONLY THERE WAS SOME WAY WE COULD MOVE AROUND IN THIS SECTOR WITHOUT RUNNIN' INTO THE NEUTRON STORM AGAIN.
LIKE WITH A CLOAKING DEVICE? WE COULD RIG ONE OF THOSE.
WE CAN?!
CLOAKING DEVICE! SO NOBODY CAN SEE US?! REALLY?!
UM-- OF COURSE! SURE!
WELL, WHAT ARE YOU WAITIN' FOR? GET ON IT!

WE CAN DO THIS, RIGHT?
PROBABLY.

SO IF WE CAN MAKE THE LIGHT *BEND AROUND* THE SHIP...
...IT'D BE INVISIBLE!
CYCLE ONE...

CYCLE TWO...
THIS FIELD GENERATOR SHOULD WARP THE LIGHT RIGHT AROUND THE SHIP'S HULL.

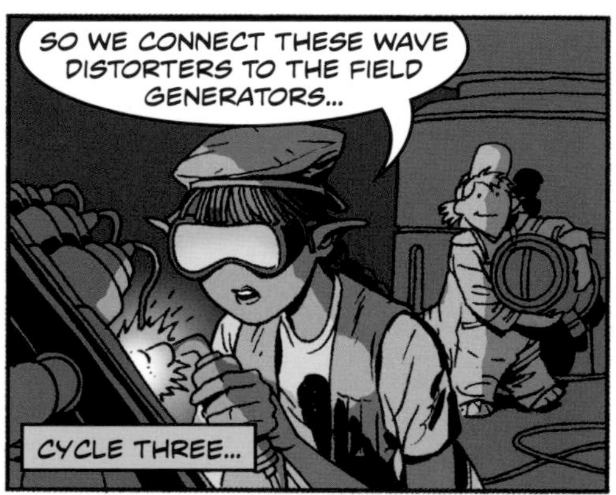
SO WE CONNECT THESE WAVE DISTORTERS TO THE FIELD GENERATORS...
CYCLE THREE...

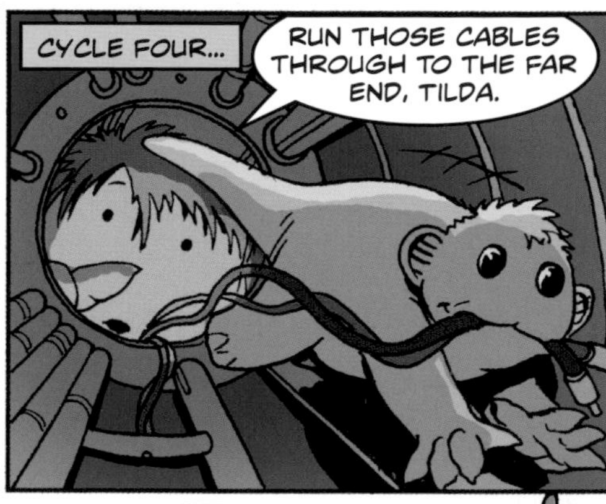
CYCLE FOUR...
RUN THOSE CABLES THROUGH TO THE FAR END, TILDA.

CYCLE FIVE...
MOVE THAT ASSEMBLY OVER TO THE PORT BAY, FELLAS. BUT EASY DOES IT!
...AND THE SYSTEM TESTED OUT PERFECT, MYK.
WE'RE BACK IN BUSINESS!

LET'S TAKE A PEEK OUTSIDE THIS ROCK YARD WE BEEN HIDIN' IN, CRUSTY.
AYE, CAP'N.

AND THERE'S THE *NEUTRON STORM*, ***WAITIN'*** FOR US TO FINALLY POKE OUR NOSE OUT OF THIS ASTEROID FIELD.
LET'S ***GIVE 'EM*** WHAT THEY WANT!

COMMANDER, WE'VE JUST ***SPOTTED*** THE *QUASAR TORRENT!*
AT LAST! READY ***PHOTON CANNONS!***
THEY'RE ***HAILING*** US, SIR!
NEUTRON STORM, THIS IS THE CAPTAIN OF THE *QUASAR TORRENT*. ***DON'T SHOOT!*** WE ***GIVE UP!*** WE'RE TURNING OURSELVES IN!
WHA-?!?

HA! IT SEEMS THESE FOOLS HAVE SEEN THE ERROR OF THEIR WAYS! HOLD FIRE, ENSIGN...
...AND PREPARE FOR CAPTURE!

SHE'S HEADED STRAIGHT FOR US, CAP'N!
PERFECT!

FIRE UP OUR NEW TOY, LADIES!
INITIATING CLOAKING SEQUENCE...

...FIVE... FOUR...
...THREE... TWO...

...ONE...
LOCKED ON TARGET, COMMANDER!
PROCEED WITH CAPTURE.

WAIT! WHERE'D IT GO?!?

YOU LOST OUR TARGET?! TRACKING-- REPORT!

AW, THIS IS BEAUTIFUL!

WE'VE LOST ALL TRACE OF THE QUASAR TORRENT, COMMANDER!
THEY CAN'T JUST DISAPPEAR--
...CAN THEY?!?
HA! HA! HA!

WE'RE *RIGHT UNDER THEIR NOSE*, AND THEY *CAN'T FIND US!*
LET'S *CIRCLE 'EM* FOR A WHILE LONGER, BOYS-- I *LIKE* THIS!

WE WANDER THROUGH THE INKY BLACK...
ZZZT
I'M PICKING UP A DISTURBANCE ON THE HULL OF THE SHIP, SIR!
ARE THEY FIRING ON US?!
IT'S NOT POWERFUL ENOUGH TO BE A WEAPON.
ZZZT
...IN SEARCH OF TREASURE NEAR AND FAR...
HIDY-HIDY YO-YO-YO...
HIDY-HIDY YO!

FELLAS, CHECK OUT THE VIEW OF THE NEUTRON STORM'S STARBOARD SIDE!!!
HA! HA! HA! HA! HA!
THE QUASAR TORRENT WAS HERE!

OKAY, ENOUGH FUN AND GAMES. LET'S LEAVE THESE DOPES IN OUR DUST!
AYE, CAP'N!
FAR RIM IS OURS FOR THE TAKING NOW, BOYS!
THE QUASA
TORREN
WAS

AND A HIDY-HIDY...
YO-YO-YO!

THEM TWO GIRLS ARE HYSTERICAL!
GENIUSES, I TELL YA!
MECHANICS-- REPORT TO THE BRIDGE!

NOW WHAT?
YOU DON'T THINK WE'RE IN TROUBLE FOR THAT PRANK, DO YA?

UM...SORRY, GUYS.
REALLY, WE WERE JUST JOKIN' AROU--
THERE THEY ARE!

HURRAY! HURRAY! HURRAY!

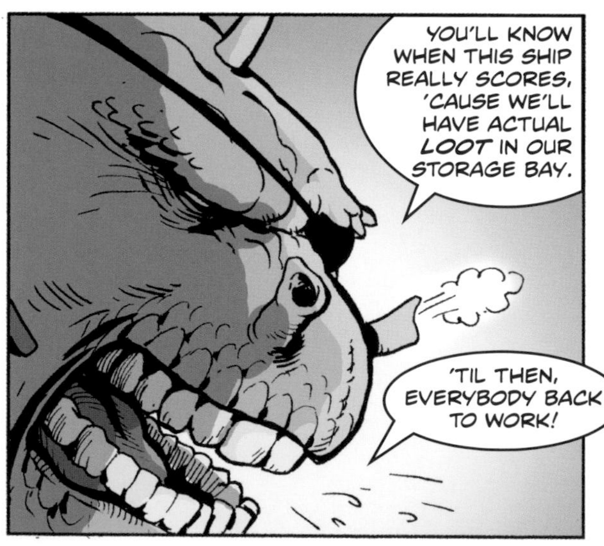

WHAT A GRUMP!
I'LL BE IN MY CABIN. DON'T NOBODY DISTURB ME.
THAT GUY'S GOT A LOT OF NERVE! AND AFTER WE INVENTED A WAY TO SAVE THIS WHOLE OPERATION!

AND WHAT DID HE DO TO MAKE THIS A SUCCESS? THE ONLY THING HE'S GOOD AT IS SHOUTIN' ORDERS AND CALLIN' US BUMS!
UM... ROX, MAYBE YOU SHOULDN'T...
YEAH! HE DOES DO THAT!

AH, WELL. WE'RE STILL THE BEST CREW OF SPACE BUCCANEERS IN THE INKY BLACK...

...RIGHT, FELLAS?!
YEAH!

...EVEN IF OUR CAPTAIN IS A GROUCHY, GREEDY, KNOW-NOTHING!
HA! HA! HA!

CHAPTER 5

WE'RE PICKIN UP A CRAFT ON THE SCOPE, CAP'N. LOOKS LIKE IT COULD BE A *QUARKCORP FREIGHTER!*
GREAT! LET'S GET ON 'ER TRAIL. *BATTLE STATIONS,* FELLAS!

QUARKCORP

ENGINEERING CREW, STAND BY FOR TRACTOR BEAM ACTIVATION.

SYSTEM CHECK IS GOOD. ALL BEAM GENERATORS ARE PRIMED FOR FULL CAPACITY.

INITIATE SNARING SEQUENCE.
WE'RE LOCKED ONTO THE TARGET.

WE *GOT IT*, CAP'N!
LET'S *REEL 'ER IN!*

ALL HANDS GRAB YOUR WEAPONS AND PREPARE TO SECURE OUR NEW PLAYMATE!

...EXCEPT FOR *ROX*.

I DON'T SEE ANY PROBLEMS DOWN HERE. AND WHY'S HE GOTTA HAVE THIS FIXED ***RIGHT NOW?*** WE ***BARELY EVER*** USE AIRLOCK FIVE!

EVERYBODY ELSE IS SECURING THAT FREIGHTER. I'M MISSING ALL THE ***FUN!***

5

UMMM--
A LITTLE.
NOT AS COLD AS IT'S *GONNA* BE.

WH-WHAT DO MEAN?
SPEAKIN' AS A "GROUCHY, GREEDY, KNOW-NOTHING," I CAN TELL YOU THAT YOU'VE BECOME A REAL THORN IN MY SIDE.
YOU AND YOUR PAL STEAL MY THUNDER... MAKE ME LOOK BAD IN FRONT OF THE CREW.

I THINK IT'S TIME YOU LEFT THE *QUASAR TORRENT*...
WHOOP!
WHOOP!
...AND I CAME DOWN HERE TO SEE YOU OFF.
WARNING: AIRLOCK OPENING IN 300 MILLICYCLES

SORRY THE REST OF THE CREW'S NOT HERE TO SAY GOODBYE. THEY'RE KINDA BUSY RIGHT NOW.
GEE, I SHOULDA GOT YOU A SPACESUIT FOR A GOIN'-AWAY PRESENT--
IT'S PRETTY *CHILLY* WHERE YOU'RE HEADED.

YOU WOULDN'T! YOU CAN'T JUST SHOOT ME OUT INTO SPACE!!!
TH-THINK OF THE RANSOM MONEY YOU'LL NEVER SEE!
RANSOM! HA!
I SNATCHED YOU SO'S I COULD GET YOUR OLD MAN TO SIGN UP AS OUR MECHANIC...
...BUT YOU, AND ESPECIALLY YOUR FRIEND, TURNED OUT TO BE BETTER WRENCH-BENDERS THAN HE EVER WAS.
YOU NEVER EVEN TALKED TO MY PARENTS, DID YOU?
IN FACT, YOUR FRIEND'S SO GOOD...
...SEEMS LIKE WE DON'T NEED YOU AT ALL!
MISS POPULARITY--
THE CREW'S GONNA BE AWFUL SAD WHEN THEY HEAR ABOUT YOUR "ACCIDENT" WHILE REPAIRIN' AIRLOCK FIVE.

HEY. THERE IS SOMETHING GOIN' ON WITH AIRLOCK FIVE. IT JUST STARTED ITS PURGE SEQUENCE!
ALERT!
AIRLOCK 5
ROX SHOULDN'T BE HANDLING THIS ON HER OWN. IT'S DANGEROUS. I'D BETTER SEE IF SHE NEEDS A HAND.

WITH THE CHAOS ON THE SHIP RIGHT NOW, I DON'T LIKE LEAVIN' THE PUPS ALONE. SOMEBODY MIGHT WANDER IN HERE.
I'LL JUST BRING 'EM ALONG.

C'MON, YOU GUYS. YOU'RE GOIN' FOR A RIDE!
MEEP!
MEEP!
MEEP!

HEY, ZAM! YOU AND ROX SHOULD HEAD DOWN TO THE LOADING BAY AND GRAB SOME LOOT.
CAN'T. GOT A SITUATION DOWN IN AIRLOCK FIVE. I'M TAKING SOME EQUIPMENT DOWN THERE NOW.

KEEP DOWN, YOU GUYS! WE'RE ALMOST THERE.

CAP'N?! I THOUGHT YOU'D BE WITH THE OTHERS!
%#&@! I TOLD YOU TO STAY PUT!
UMM...WELL... I GOT AN ALERT MESSAGE AND THOUGHT THERE MIGHT BE A...

LET...

...HER...

...GO!

SO NOW I'M GONNA HAVE TROUBLE WITH YOU, TOO?

YOU SURE ARE!
KLONK!
OW!

OOF!
DON'T WORRY, ROX...
WHOOSH!!

ZAM! WATCH OUT...
KLONK!
...I'LL HAVE YOU OUTTA THERE...

...AS SOON AS...
...REMEMBER HE'S GOT...

...A BLASTER!

OH...RIGHT!
I DIDN'T WANT YOU INVOLVED IN THIS, KID...

MEEP?
...BUT WHAT THE HECK...

MEEP!
MEEP!
...LOOKS LIKE I'M GONNA NEED *TWO* NEW MECHANICS!
MEEP!

!!!
GLAR!
SNARG!
ROWL!
SNORT!
WHAT THE-- ?!?
YEOW!
HOLD ON, ROX...

SNARG!
GLAR!
ROWL!!
OW!
OUCH!
...I'LL GET YOU OUT!
HURRY! THE LOCK'S GONNA OPEN IN...

...12 MILLICYCLES!
AIRLOCK OPENING IN:
00:12

UM...AH...ACCESS LOCK PROTOCOL!
AIRLOCK OPENING

THEN...UM... DELETE SEQUENCE...
00:08

HURRY, ZAM!

PLEASE ENTER YOUR SECURITY CODE.
AIRLOCK OPENING IN:
00:02
?!? SECURITY CODE?!?

OH, WELL...!
SMASH!

THAT *WORKED?!?*

Y-YOU *STOPPED* IT?!?

YEAH, BUT NOW HOW DO I *OPEN THE DOOR* TO GET YOU OUT?!

FILTHY SPACE RATS!

OW!

THEY'RE NOT RATS! *YOU'RE* THE RAT!

YOU BETTER NOT HURT THEM!

ME HURT *THEM?!?*

OUCH!

I THINK I HEAR THE CREW COMIN'!
BACK IN THE CASE, BABIES! NOW!

WHAT'S ALL THE NOISE ABOUT DOWN HERE? WE WAS JUST PASSIN' BY AND--

RED MYK TRIED TO KILL ROX!
WHAT?!?

HE WAS GONNA SHOOT ME OUT OF THE AIRLOCK!
IT'S TRUE! I STOPPED HIM BUT HE RAN OFF AND--

THAT DIRTY--!!!

THREATENIN' INNOCENT GIRLS! THAT NO GOOD--!
I'VE HAD ENOUGH OF THAT CREEP!
I'LL TELL THE OTHERS! ONCE THEY HEAR ABOUT THIS--!

ALL HANDS BE ON THE LOOK OUT FOR RED MYK!
BRING THAT BUM TO THE GALLEY-- ONE WAY OR ANOTHER!
SO IT'S MUTINY!
THOSE UNGRATEFUL SCUMBAGS!

THAT'S THE THANKS I GET FOR TURNIN' A BUNCHA UNEMPLOYED SPACE TRASH INTO THE MOST FEARED PIRATES IN THE GALAXY!
NOW I GOTTA HIDE FROM MY OWN #$%& CREW...

...ALL 'CAUSE OF THOSE TWO BRATS!

I CAN'T HIDE FOREVER ON THIS SHIP...
ROX AND ZAM'S PLACE

...BUT THE GIRLS' QUARTERS SHOULD BE THE LAST PLACE THEY'LL LOOK FOR ME.
CREW STAY OUT!!
GIRLS NEED PRIVACY!

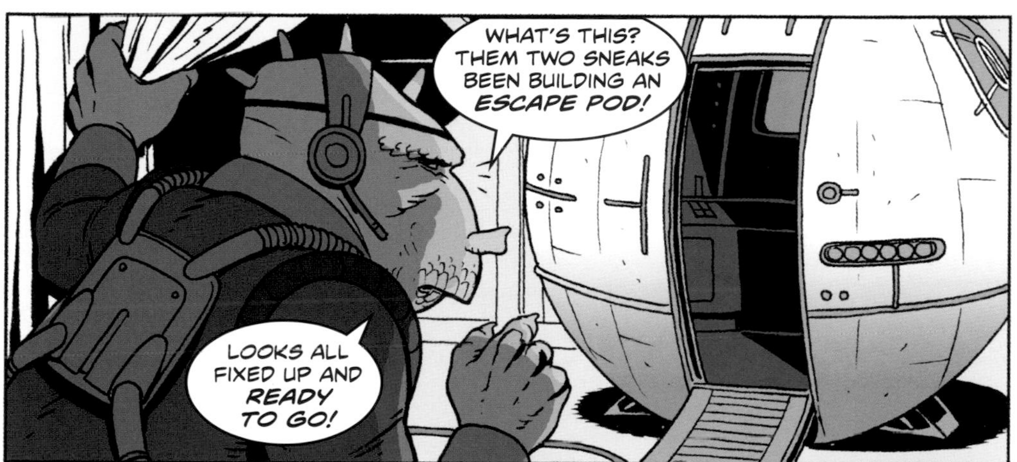
WHAT'S THIS? THEM TWO SNEAKS BEEN BUILDING AN *ESCAPE POD!*
LOOKS ALL FIXED UP AND *READY TO GO!*

SORRY, GIRLS...

...THIS RIDE'S GOT *MY NAME* ON IT NOW.
SHOOOFF

MUTINY!
I'LL REMEMBER HOW THIS CREW TURNED ON ME!

AND THOSE TWO GIRLS COST ME MY SHIP!

I'LL FIND A WAY TO MAKE 'EM ALL PAY...

...IF IT'S THE LAST THING I EVER DO!

I DON'T UNDERSTAND IT! WE'VE BEEN ALL OVER THIS SHIP, AND THERE'S NO SIGN OF RED MYK!
FINALLY *FREE!* THANKS, ZAM.
SORRY. I HAD TO HOTWIRE THE DOOR.
HE'S GOTTA BE AROUND *SOME-WHERE!*

HEY! DIDN'T THERE USED TO BE AN OLD ESCAPE POD IN STORAGE DOWN IN ENGINEERING?
THAT BROKEN-DOWN, OLD THING? HE COULDN'T...
!!!

UM...WELL... MAYBE HE *COULD*...
W-WE FIXED IT UP A WHILE BACK.

THE SHIP'S COMPUTER SHOWS A DISCHARGE FROM A TRASH PORT DOWN IN THAT AREA JUST A LITTLE WHILE AGO.
THAT MUSTA BEEN HIM! *HA!* HE'S *TRASH* ALL RIGHT!

THEY'RE ALL OVER THE PLACE!

THERE MUSTA BEEN A BUNCH OF 'EM SCUFFLIN' AROUND!

THAT'S FUNNY--WE DIDN'T SEE A THING!

NOPE! --HEH-- NO SPACE GREMLINS SINCE WE'VE BEEN HERE.

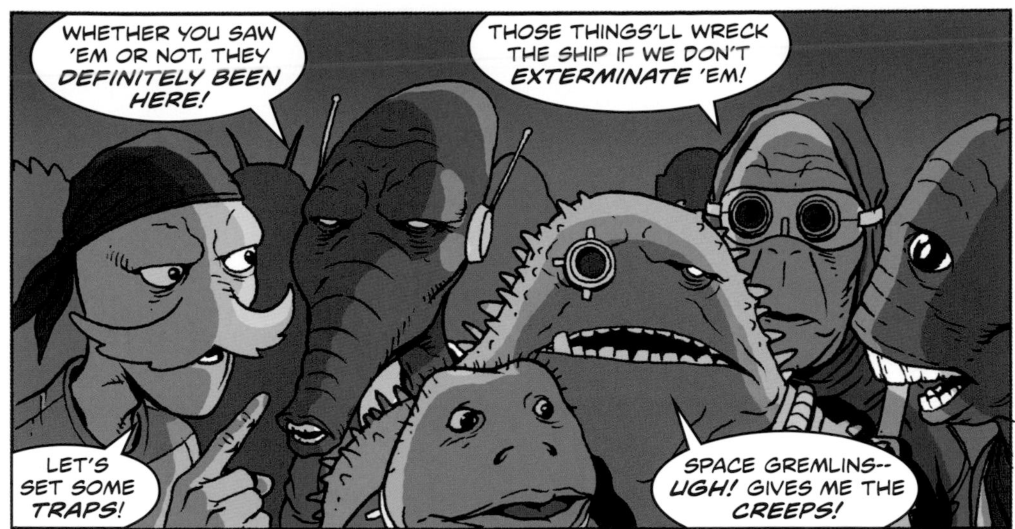

IF YOU GIRLS ARE SQUEAMISH ABOUT HURTIN' CRITTERS. DON'T WORRY--*WE'LL* TAKE CARE OF THE PROBLEM!

LET'S GET TO WORK, FELLAS!

ONCE WE FIND 'EM...

...WE'LL *GET RID* OF EVERY LAST ONE OF THE DIRTY *LITTLE PESTS!*

CHAPTER 6

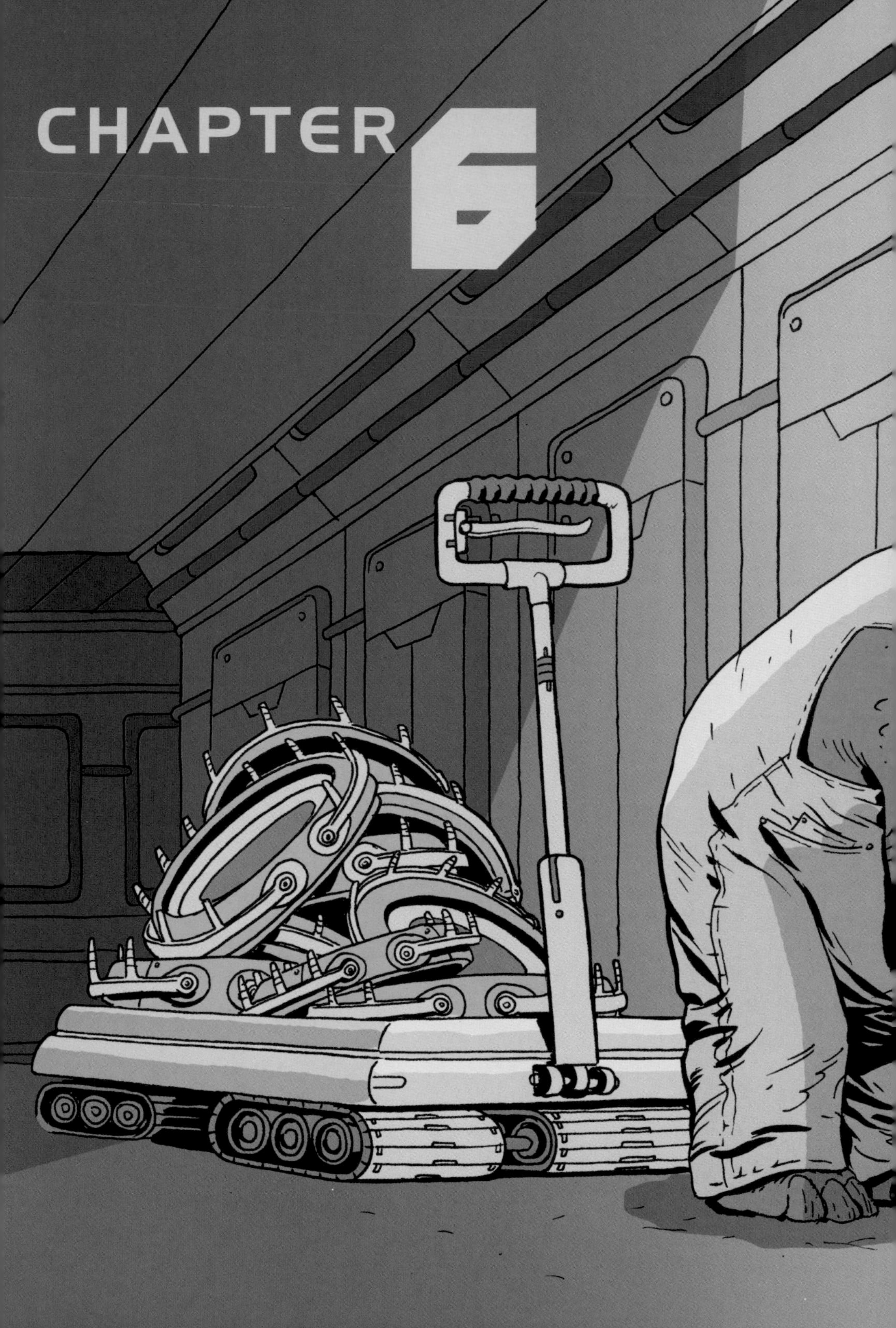

THESE OUGHTA DO THE TRICK!
WHATCHA GOT THERE, SPYK?

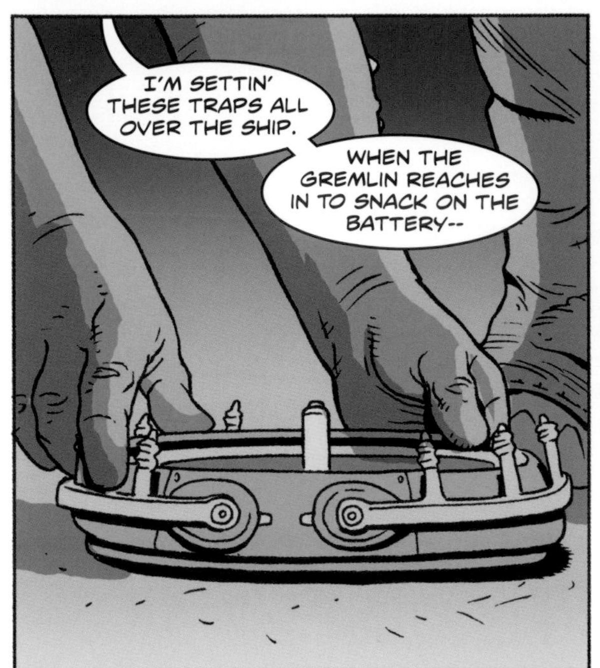
I'M SETTIN' THESE TRAPS ALL OVER THE SHIP.
WHEN THE GREMLIN REACHES IN TO SNACK ON THE BATTERY--

ZAP! IT DISINTEGRATES THE LITTLE PEST! COOL, HUH?!
EH... YEAH... COOL.

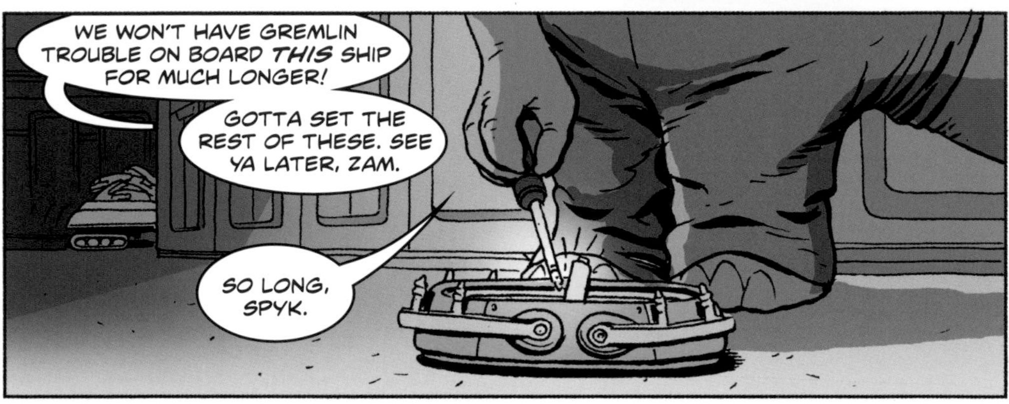
WE WON'T HAVE GREMLIN TROUBLE ON BOARD THIS SHIP FOR MUCH LONGER!
GOTTA SET THE REST OF THESE. SEE YA LATER, ZAM.
SO LONG, SPYK.

KA-ZAP!

THAT'S ONE DISARMED. HOW MANY MORE TO GO?

WHAT IF THE PUPS ESCAPE FROM OUR QUARTERS AND START WANDERING THE SHIP AGAIN?
ROX AND I NEED TO COME UP WITH A PLAN TO KEEP 'EM SAFE.

HERE'S TO A NEW ERA FOR THE CREW O' THE *QUASAR TORRENT*.

I DECLARE THIS SHIP A ***RED MYK-FREE ZONE!***
HA! HA! DARN RIGHT!
IT'S GONNA BE GREAT AROUND HERE WITHOUT HIM RIDIN' US CONSTANTLY!

YEAH. WITHOUT MYK HERE, THIS IS THE FIRST QUIET DAY ZAM AND I HAVE HAD SINCE YOU FIRST KIDNAPPED US!
KIDNAPPED?!

DID YOU SAY ***KIDNAPPED?!***
WHADDAYA MEAN?
YOU KNOW-- SINCE WE GOT TRICKED ON BOARD THE *TORRENT* AND HAULED AWAY FROM HOME.

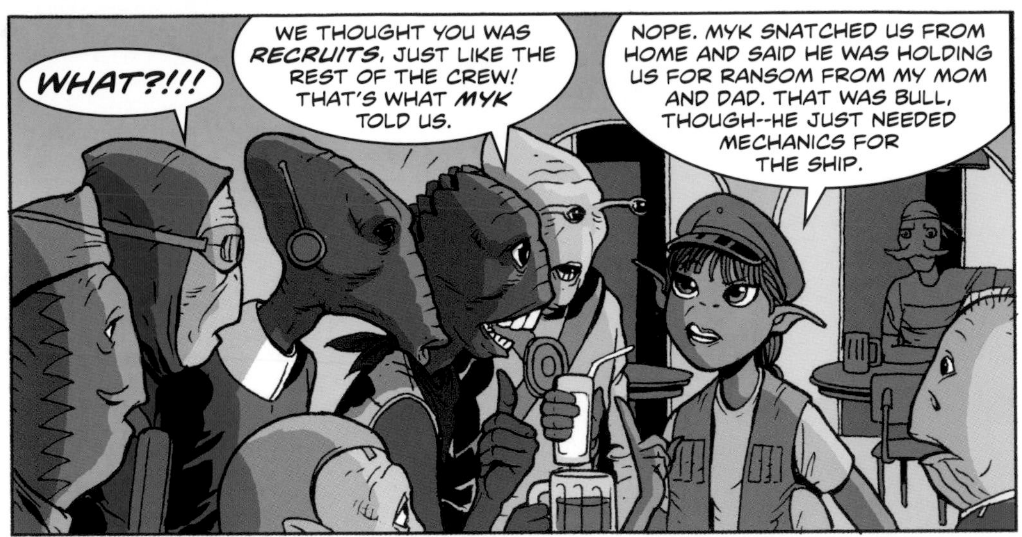
WHAT?!!!
WE THOUGHT YOU WAS RECRUITS, JUST LIKE THE REST OF THE CREW! THAT'S WHAT MYK TOLD US.
NOPE. MYK SNATCHED US FROM HOME AND SAID HE WAS HOLDING US FOR RANSOM FROM MY MOM AND DAD. THAT WAS BULL, THOUGH--HE JUST NEEDED MECHANICS FOR THE SHIP.

WHY THAT NO GOOD, DIRTY--!
BEIN' A PIRATE IS ONE THING, BUT BEIN' A KIDNAPPER--THAT'S LOW!

ZAM AND I JUST ASSUMED YOU GUYS KNEW ALL ABOUT--
HEY, ROX! WE GOTTA TALK!

ZAM, YOU WON'T BELIEVE WHAT I JUST--
C'MON! WE GOTTA DEAL WITH AN EMERGENCY WITH...UM...THE THINGIES...
THINGIES? WHAT THINGIES?!

THE TINY THINGIES!
OH, THOSE THINGIES! RIGHT!
CATCH YOU GUYS LATER.

...AND SPYK WAS SETTING DISINTEGRATOR TRAPS ALL OVER THE SHIP. WE NEED A PLAN TO GET THE PUPS OFF THE *TORRENT* BEFORE THEY END UP AS ***ATOMIC ASH!***

OFF THE SHIP?! HOW? WITH THE POD GONE WE CAN'T EVEN GET ***OURSELVES*** OFF THE SHIP!

ALTHOUGH, NOW THAT WE'VE FOUND OUT THE CREW WASN'T IN ON OUR KIDNAPPING-- WELL...

...MAYBE THEY'LL UNDERSTAND IF WE JUST TELL THEM ABOUT THE PUPS!

MAYBE THE CREW WILL LET US GO... AND LET US TAKE THE BABIES WITH US?

WE HAD NO IDEA YOU TWO WAS ***KIDNAPPED***.

ONCE WE FOUND OUT, WE ALL AGREED WE GOTTA DO THE RIGHT THING...

...WE GOTTA TAKE YOU BACK TO YOUR HOME.

WHA--!!!

R-REALLY?!
WE'RE LEAVING THE QUASAR TORRENT?!
YOU TWO DON'T BELONG OUT HERE, ON THE RUN WITH A BUNCHA SPACE BUMS.

YOU GUYS ARE THE BEST!
SNIFF!
AW...
WHY DON'T YA GO USE THE COMLINK TO CALL YOUR FOLKS--LET 'EM KNOW YOU'LL BE COMIN' HOME.

...AND SO ZAM AND I SHOULD BE BACK THERE IN JUST A FEW CYCLES!
OH, ROX! THAT'S WONDERFUL! WE'VE BEEN SO WORRIED!
WE WERE AFRAID WE'D NEVER SEE YOU AGAIN!

RED MYK AND HIS BAND OF NO-GOOD SPACE THUGS! I SHOULD NEVER HAVE LET THEM LAND HERE IN THE FIRST PLACE!
IS ANYBODY LISTENING IN ON US NOW, ROX?
NO. THEY THOUGHT I'D WANT TO CALL YOU IN PRIVATE.
GOOD! SO I'LL ALERT THE SECTOR SPACE PATROL ABOUT THIS. MAYBE THEY COULD CATCH THE TORRENT--YOU KNOW--AFTER THEY DROP YOU GIRLS OFF SAFE.

WHAT? NO, DAD! DON'T!
THEY'RE PIRATES, ROX! THEY CAN'T BE LEFT TO ROAM AROUND RAIDING SHIPS AND KIDNAPPING FOLKS!

THEY'RE GOOD GUYS! THEY'RE BRINGING US HOME!
WE HAVE TO LET THE AUTHORITIES KNOW ABOUT THIS!

ONCE YOU'RE HERE SAFE AND SOUND, THE SPACE PATROL CAN SWEEP IN AND CAPTURE THE BUNCH OF THEM!

YOUR MOM'S RIGHT, ROX. THIS IS THE PERFECT CHANCE TO STOP THOSE THUGS!
NO, MAMA! YOU CAN'T!

B-BUT THEY'RE MY FRIENDS!

DON'T BE SILLY, ROX! THEY KIDNAPPED YOU!
THAT WAS RED MYK! THE CREW DIDN'T DO IT!
DON'T WORRY ABOUT THIS, ROXIE. WE'LL TAKE CARE OF EVERYTHING. YOU JUST MAKE IT HOME TO US SAFE AND SOUND.

I WON'T BETRAY MY FRIENDS.
BELIEVE ME, THEY'RE NOT YOUR FRIENDS, ROX!

PROMISE YOU WON'T CALL THE SECTOR PATROL ON THEM!
ROX, THIS IS NOT YOUR DECISION TO MAKE. YOU HAVE TO TRUST US ON THIS!

I-I CAN'T DO THAT.
OF COURSE YOU CAN...

...AND YOU DON'T THINK YOU CAN TRUST YOUR OWN *PARENTS?*

I *DO*-- I TRUST THEY'LL DO WHAT *THEY THINK* IS THE RIGHT THING...

...BUT WHAT THEY THINK IS THE RIGHT THING IS REALLY THE *WRONG THING!*

THIS WOULDA BEEN THE PERFECT CHANCE TO GET THE PUPS OFF THE SHIP SAFE AND SOUND.
I KNOW! I'M SO CONFUSED!
I WANNA SEE MY *PARENTS*! I WANT THE *BABIES* SAFE! I WANT THE *CREW* SAFE!
HEY...
...Y'KNOW WHAT, ROX--

I'M GONNA ***MISS*** WORKING ON THE *QUASAR TORRENT* ONCE WE LEAVE.

YEAH. AND BEING A PIRATE IS A LOT MORE INTERESTING THAN BEING STUCK ON AN ASTEROID IN THE MIDDLE OF NOWHERE.

SIGH

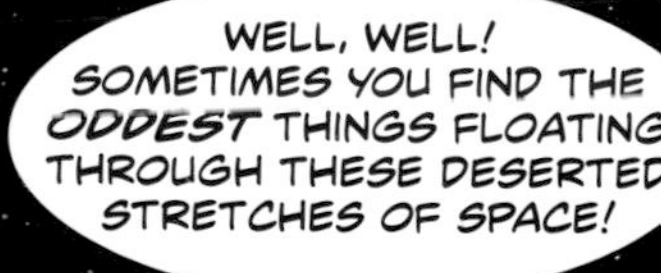
WELL, WELL! SOMETIMES YOU FIND THE ***ODDEST*** THINGS FLOATING THROUGH THESE DESERTED STRETCHES OF SPACE!
GRRRR! JUST MY LUCK THAT ***YOU GUYS*** ARE THE FIRST SHIP I RUN INTO OUT HERE.

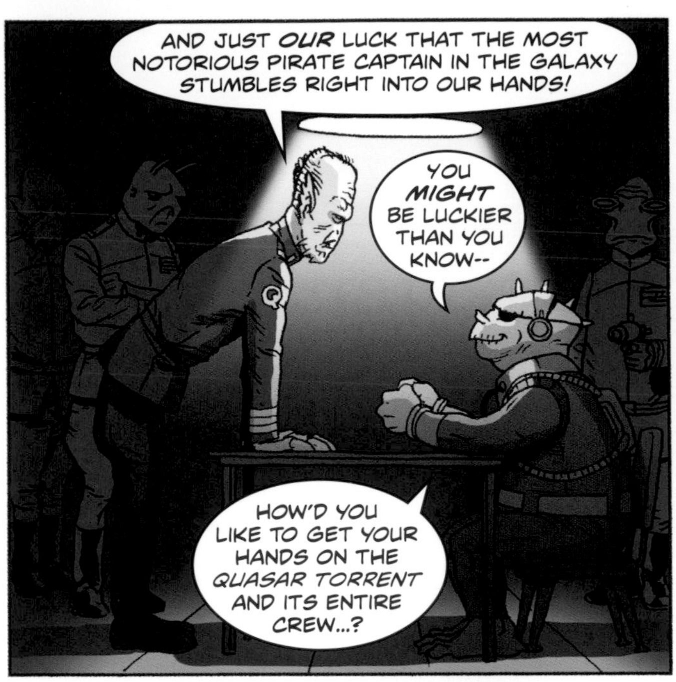
AND JUST OUR LUCK THAT THE MOST NOTORIOUS PIRATE CAPTAIN IN THE GALAXY STUMBLES RIGHT INTO OUR HANDS!
YOU MIGHT BE LUCKIER THAN YOU KNOW--
HOW'D YOU LIKE TO GET YOUR HANDS ON THE QUASAR TORRENT AND ITS ENTIRE CREW...?

...FOR THE PRICE OF LETTING ME WALK, OF COURSE...
...AND MAYBE A SMALL CONSULTANT'S FEE!

I'M NOT IN THE HABIT OF MAKING DEALS WITH PIRATES.
FINE. THEN EXPLAIN TO THE SUITS AT QUARKCORP HOW YOU BLEW A CHANCE TO HOOK THE TORRENT-- AND DISCOVER HOW THEIR NEW CLOAKING TECHNOLOGY WORKS.

CLOAKING! THAT'S HOW THEY ESCAPED US?!
IT IS. AND MORE IMPORTANTLY--I CAN TELL YOU HOW IT WORKS...
...AND HOW TO COUNTERACT IT!

HMMM. AN INTRIGUING NOTION.
TELL ME MORE.

SO WITH RED MYK GONE WE HAVE TO DECIDE WHAT OUR NEXT MOVE IS GONNA BE.
Y'KNOW, WE GOT ENOUGH LOOT ON THIS SHIP THAT WE CAN ALL *RETIRE*, IF WE WANNA!
RETIRE? PHOOEY! RED MYK WAS THE GUY THAT CARED ABOUT LOOT! I THOUGHT WE WERE HERE TO *HASSLE QUARK-CORP!*
YEAH! LOOT WON'T BUY BACK THE LIVES WE LED *BEFORE QUARK'S GATE* OPENED!
NO-- BUT WE CAN BUY *BETTER* ONES!

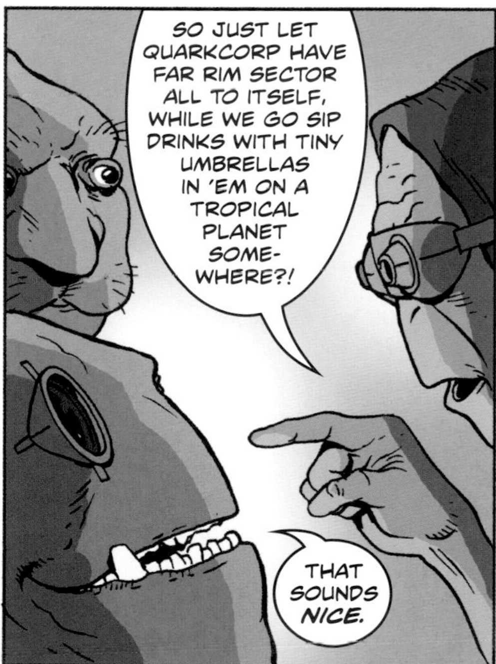
SO JUST LET QUARKCORP HAVE FAR RIM SECTOR ALL TO ITSELF, WHILE WE GO SIP DRINKS WITH TINY UMBRELLAS IN 'EM ON A TROPICAL PLANET SOME-WHERE?!
THAT SOUNDS *NICE.*

WHAT SOUNDS *NICER* IS CHASING QUARKCORP OUTTA FAR RIM SO IT BELONGS TO *US* AGAIN!
YOU BET! I WANT MY *OLD LIFE* BACK!

AS LONG AS THERE'S MONEY TO BE MADE FROM CONTROLLIN' THAT WORMHOLE, QUARKCORP WILL *NEVER* LEAVE FAR RIM!
HA! WE AIN'T GOT THE MUSCLE TO CHASE QUARKCORP OUTTA OUR SECTOR!

HEY, FELLAS! THE SCOPE'S PICKIN' UP A BIG SHIP IN THE DISTANCE. MIGHT BE THE *NEUTRON STORM*!

DANG! EVERYBODY TO THEIR STATIONS. ***START THE ENGINES!***

ROX AND ZAM--WE GOT THE *NEUTRON STORM* ON OUR TAIL AGAIN! ***FIRE UP THE CLOAKING DEVICE!***
YIKES!
WE'LL GET RIGHT ON IT!

I WONDER HOW THE NEUTRON STORM FOUND US THIS TIME?
THIS DEAD MOON HAS ALWAYS BEEN OUR FAVORITE PLACE TO LAY LOW AFTER A JOB. NOW WE'LL HAVE TO FIND A NEW HIDEOUT!
DON'T WORRY ABOUT THAT NOW. WE GOTTA MOVE!
ENGAGE CLOAKING DEVICE, GIRLS!
WILL DO!
OKAY, FELLAS. LET'S JUST SNEAK AWAY FROM 'EM-- NICE AND QUIET!

SCOPE IS TRACKING THE *QUASAR TORRENT*, COMMANDER.
WAIT! THEY'VE ***DISAPPEARED***, SIR!
I ***KNEW*** WE'D FIND 'EM HERE...
...AND IT'S GOIN' DOWN JUST LIKE I TOLD YA!

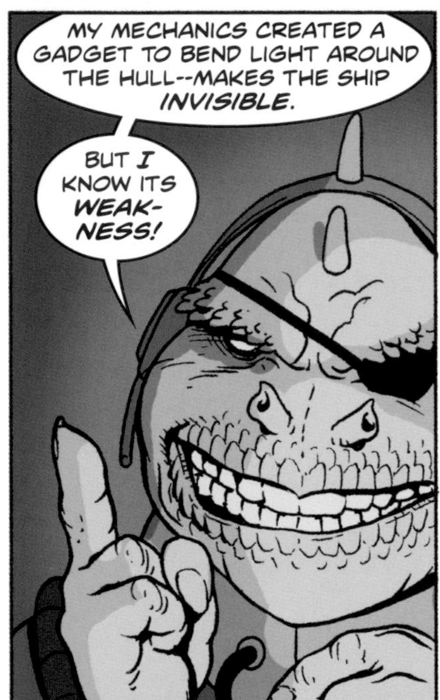
MY MECHANICS CREATED A GADGET TO BEND LIGHT AROUND THE HULL--MAKES THE SHIP *INVISIBLE*.
BUT *I* KNOW ITS ***WEAK-NESS!***

YOUR BARGAIN HAS BEEN AGREED TO, SIR. TELL US-- *HOW DO WE FIND THE TORRENT?*
JUST SET YOUR SCOPES TO PICK UP *QUANTUM FIELD DISTORTIONS* INSTEAD OF VISIBLE LIGHT.
ENSIGN, MAKE IT SO.

RECALIBRATING, SIR...

HEY! WE'RE PICKING UP *SOMETHING...*

YOU CAN BET IT'S THE TORRENT! THEM GIR--ER--MECHANICS TOLD ME A LITTLE TOO MUCH ABOUT THEIR INVENTION--
IT DISTORTS LIGHT, BUT IT LEAVES OTHER ENERGY TRACES FROM THE SHIP UNTOUCHED.
PERFECT! THE QUASAR TORRENT IS OURS FOR THE TAKING!
ENSIGN, MOVE US IN AS CLOSE AS YOU CAN WITHOUT TIPPING THEM OFF...
...THEN PREPARE TO FIRE.
HA! LOOK AT 'EM SITTING THERE, ALL CLUELESS!
I ALMOST FEEL SORRY FOR 'EM!

THAT'S **WEIRD!**

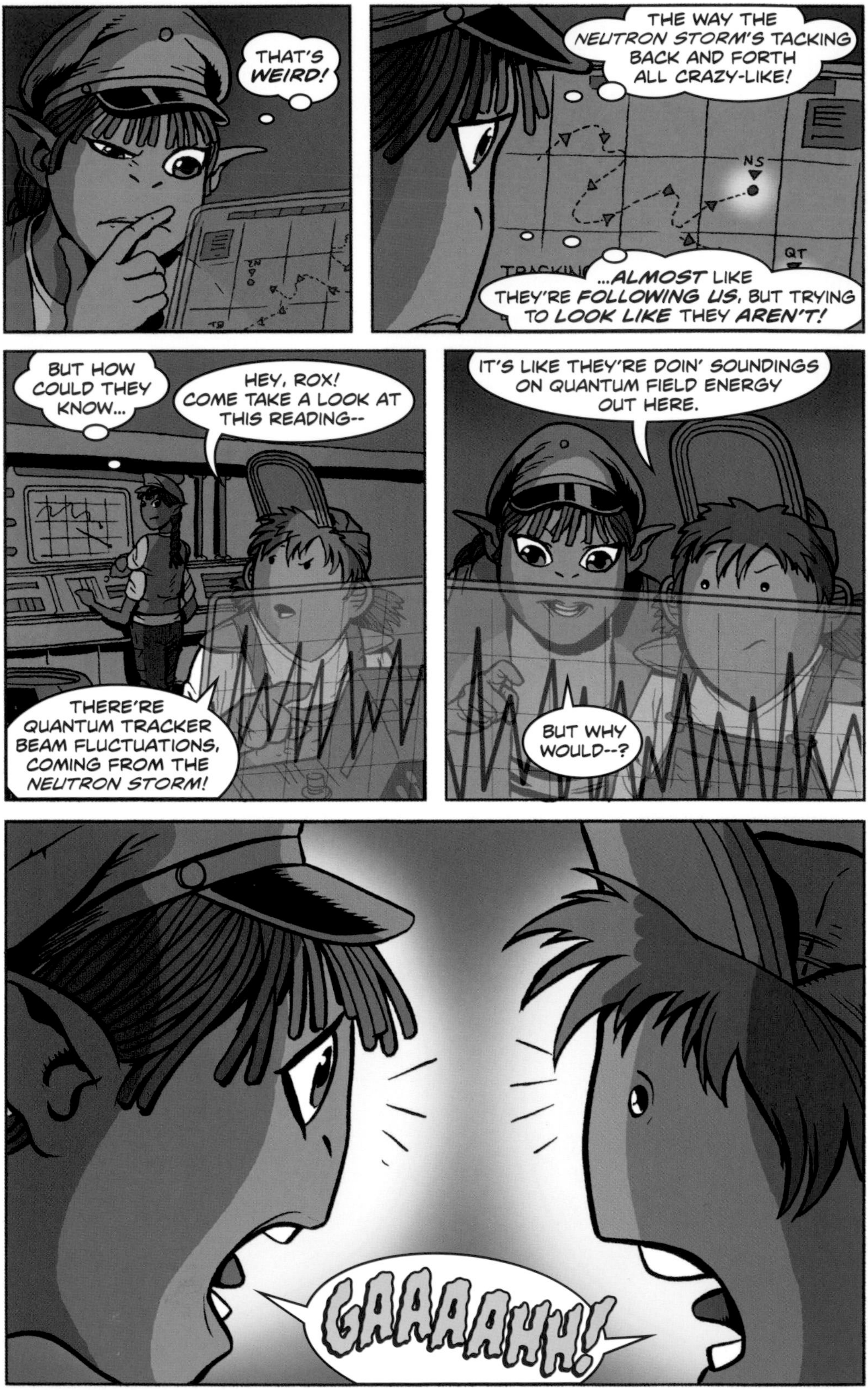

THE WAY THE *NEUTRON STORM'S* TACKING BACK AND FORTH ALL CRAZY-LIKE!
NS
QT
...**ALMOST** LIKE THEY'RE **FOLLOWING US,** BUT TRYING TO **LOOK LIKE** THEY **AREN'T!**

BUT HOW COULD THEY KNOW...
HEY, ROX! COME TAKE A LOOK AT THIS READING--
THERE'RE QUANTUM TRACKER BEAM FLUCTUATIONS, COMING FROM THE *NEUTRON STORM!*

IT'S LIKE THEY'RE DOIN' SOUNDINGS ON QUANTUM FIELD ENERGY OUT HERE.
BUT WHY WOULD--?

GAAAAHH!

BRIDGE, THIS IS ROX AND ZAM! THE NEUTRON STORM IS TRACKING US!
THEY KNOW WHERE WE ARE!
ALL POWER TO THE ENGINES! WE GOTTA GET OUTTA HERE-- NOW!
WHAT?!?
THE TORRENT'S PICKING UP SPEED, LIKE THEY'RE TRYING TO PULL AWAY FROM US!
VERY WELL. NO MORE TOYING WITH THESE SCALAWAGS!
GO STRAIGHT AT THEM!
PREPARE TO...

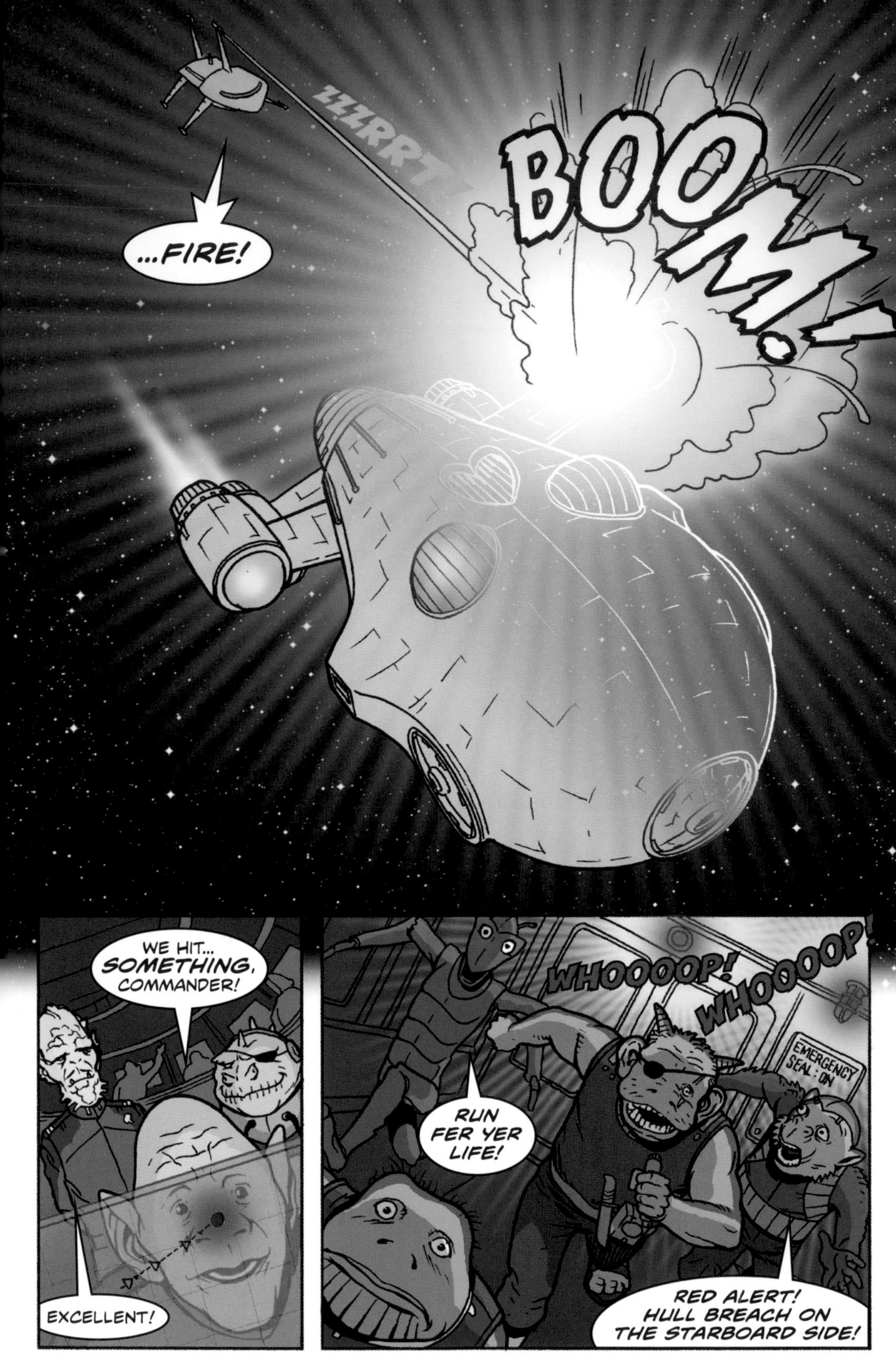
...FIRE!
ZZZRRRT
BOOM!
WE HIT... SOMETHING, COMMANDER!
EXCELLENT!
WHOOOOOP! WHOOOOOP!
EMERGENCY SEAL : ON
RUN FER YER LIFE!
RED ALERT! HULL BREACH ON THE STARBOARD SIDE!

WE CAN'T JUST *LET THEM LOOSE* ALL OVER! THE CREW WILL *SEE THEM!*

ZAM, THAT *DOESN'T MATTER* NOW! IF WE DON'T DO THIS, WE'RE *ALL* COOKED!

TILDA, HEAD TO ENGINE FOUR! *ZYK*, GO TO TO LEVEL FIVE! *TIF* AND *PEG*, FIX THE SHORT CIRCUITS UP ON THE BRIDGE!!!

GO, BABIES! *GO!*

HEY, LOOK!

GREMLINS!

THEM'S THE *LEAST* OF OUR WORRIES! *C'MON*--WE GOTTA SEAL OFF LEVEL THREE!

ANOTHER HULL BREACH IN LEVEL TWO!

ENGINE THREE IS OFFLINE!

THE CLOAKING SYSTEM IS DOWN!

W-WE CAN'T SHAKE 'EM!

I-I DON'T SEE A WAY OUTTA THIS!
MAYBE WE SHOULD ...YOU KNOW... SURRENDER?

WHAT THE--?!
GREMLINS!

AS IF WE DIDN'T HAVE ENOUGH TROUBLE RIGHT NOW!
GET THOSE THINGS OUTTA THERE!

C'MERE, YOU LITTLE--!
AXYL, WAIT...!

THE CONSOLE'S WORKIN' AGAIN!
?!?!

THEM THINGS MUSTA *FIXED* IT!
?!?!
ROX, I'M SEALING UP SOME OF THE HULL CRACKS!
ZYK AND TIF ARE REWIRING THE POWER ROUTERS!
HOW ARE YOU DOING WITH THE WELDING?
NOT GOOD! THERE'S TOO MANY FRACTURES!
I'VE GOT PEG AND JIF CUTTING SOME OF THE SHORTED CABLES!
BIL AND LONY ARE TRYING TO SALVAGE THE OXY COMPRESSORS!
THESE HYPERDRIVES ARE OVERLOADED!
THE FIRE IN STEERING IS OUTTA CONTROL!
UH OH! WE'RE LOSING THE GRAVITY GENERATORS!

AW CRAP!
LET'S FACE IT, FELLAS--WE'RE NOT GETTING OUTTA THIS SCRAPE!
ZAM, WE CAN'T KEEP UP! EVEN WITH THE BABIES, THERE ARE TOO MANY BREAKDOWNS!
IF ONLY WE COULD GET THE NEUTRON STORM OFF OUR TAIL FOR A WHILE...
...BUT THAT'S NOT GONNA HAPPEN!
W-WHAT IF WE GAVE THEM SOMETHING TO CHASE THEY WANTED EVEN MORE THAN US?!
???
GUYS! GUYS! IT'S ROX! I'VE GOT AN IDEA!
DOES IT INVOLVE US LIVING THROUGH THIS?
MAYBE!
THEN WE'RE ALL EARS!

THE *QUASAR TORRENT* IS SLOWING TO A CRAWL, CAPTAIN! SHE SEEMS TO BE DISABLED.
EXCELLENT! PREPARE TO ***FIRE*** ON HER ONCE MORE!
HEH!
WHILE SHE'S ***HELPLESS?!***
I MEAN TO ***RID THE SPACEWAYS*** OF THESE VERMIN, ENSIGN. NOW LOCK ONTO YOUR TARGET!
YEAH! KNOCK ALL THE FIGHT OUT OF 'EM!
BA-DOOM
A HIT! NICELY DONE, ENSIGN!
I-IT ***WASN'T ME,*** SIR!
THAT EXPLOSION CAME FROM ***ON BOARD THE TORRENT!***

HMM. AN INTERNAL EXPLOSION. THE *TORRENT'S* ON HER LAST LEGS, FOR SURE!

SHE'S ***SPEWING SOMETHING*** OUT INTO OPEN SPACE!

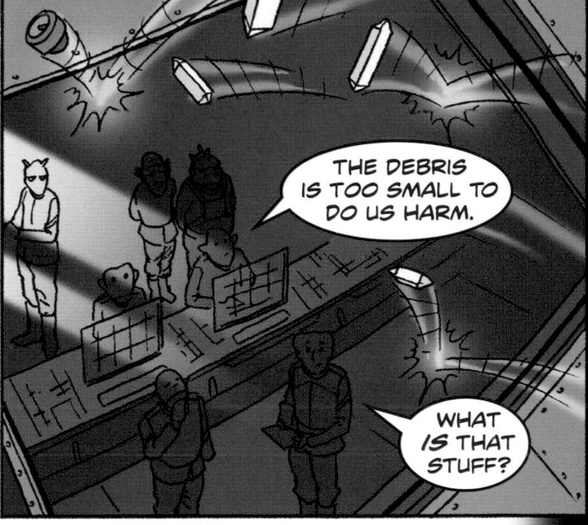

IT'S TREASURE! THEY'VE JETTISONED ALL THEIR STOLEN CARGO!!
GAAAH! ALL MY LOOT!!!

THE QUARKCORP BOARD WILL BE SO PLEASED!
I'LL MAKE ADMIRAL FOR SURE!
ACTIVATE THE TRACTOR BEAMS! OPEN THE MAIN PORT! ALL AVAILABLE HANDS TO THE LOADING DECK!
LET'S SWEEP UP AS MUCH AS WE CAN!

THEY TOOK THE BAIT!

THEY'RE LETTING US SLINK AWAY.

I GOTTA HAND IT TO YA, KID--YER IDEA ***WORKED!***

I GUESSED THEY'D BE MORE INTERESTED IN OUR ***TREASURE*** THAN IN OUR HIDES!

WE'RE NOT SAFE ***YET!*** THE *TORRENT'S* BARELY HOLDIN' TOGETHER.

WHAT'VE YOU GOT THERE, J'OH?

I FOUND THIS IN A DRAWER IN THE GALLEY.

OH.

I MISS HER, TOO.

IT'S RUSTY. THINK WE CAN GET IT WORKING AGAIN?
WE'LL SEE.
HUH.
NEW CUSTOMER. SOME OLD WRECK LIMPIN' IN HOT.
SOUNDS LIKE IT'S ON ITS LAST LEGS.
BOOM!
OUCH! THAT WAS A PRETTY ROUGH LANDING.
THINK THERE'LL BE MUCH LEFT AFTER THAT?
MAYBE. LET'S GO SEE WHAT WE CAN SALVAGE.

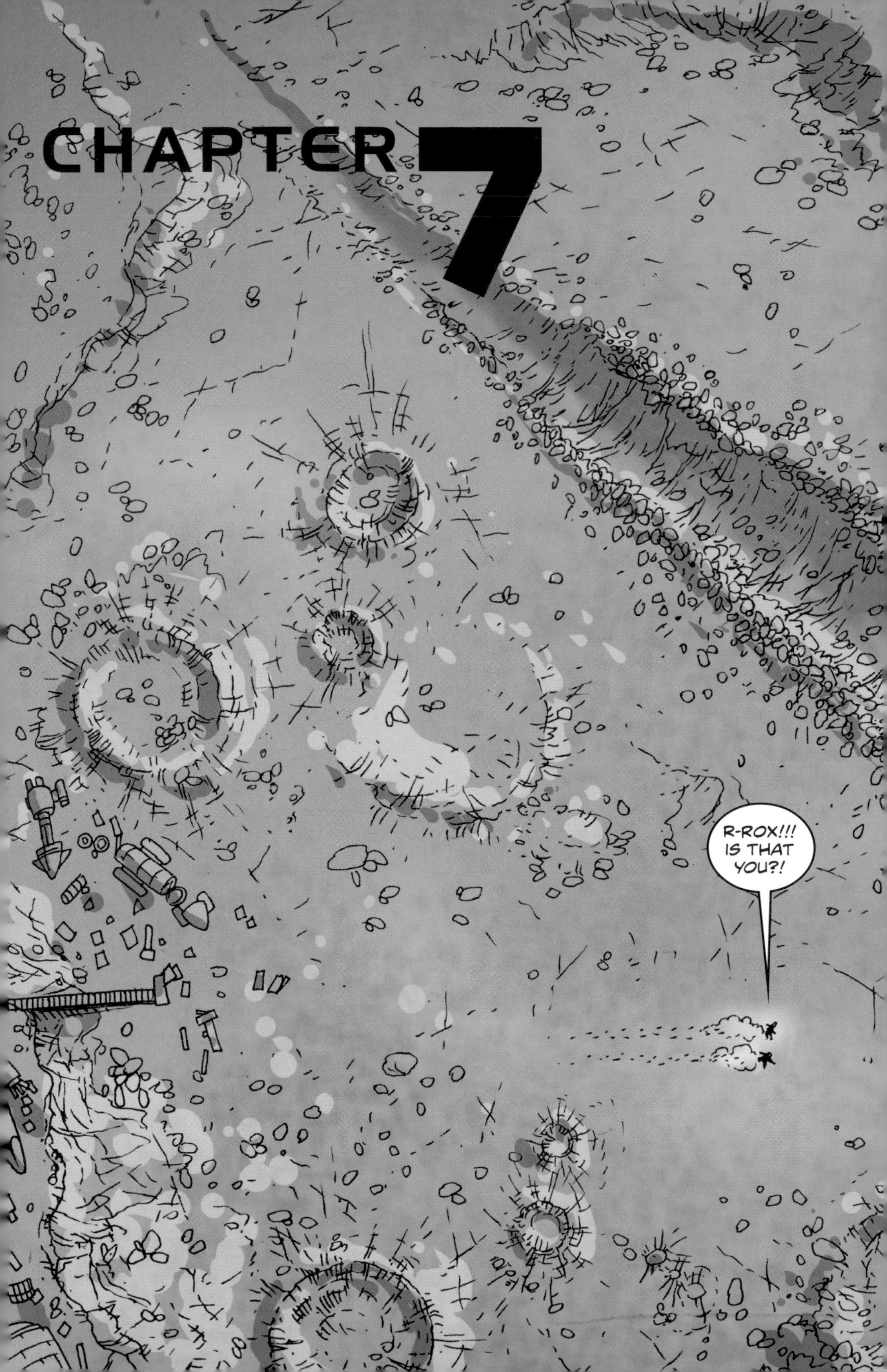
CHAPTER 7
R-ROX!!! IS THAT YOU?!

MAMA! DAD!

OH, ROX!

EVERYBODY STILL IN ONE PIECE?

YEAH-- 'LESS YOU'RE COUNTIN' THE *QUASAR TORRENT*.

--AND ZAM! OH, ZAM, IT'S GOOD TO SEE *YOU, TOO!*

IT IS?!

HA! HA! OF COURSE!

HEY, THERE'S THE ***GREMLINS*** AGAIN!!!

ALL THIS BAD LUCK-- BETCHA IT'S ***THEIR*** FAULT.

THEY'RE NOT GREMLINS! THEY'RE BABY ZOLORIANS!
WHATEVER THEY ARE, THEM THINGS WAS SCREWIN' UP THE POWER CELLS ALL OVER THE SHIP!
BUT ROX AND I MADE 'EM STOP THAT!

THAT'S RIGHT! WE TRAINED THEM! THEY WERE HELPING TO KEEP THE SHIP WORKING WELL ENOUGH TO GET US HERE!
ONE OF 'EM FIXED MY NAV CONSOLE ON THE BRIDGE!
AND I SAW ONE FIXIN' THE OXY COMPRESSOR, TOO!

THEY AIN'T GREMLINS?!
NO...

...THEY'RE LIKE ME!

GREMLINS GIVE ME THE CREEPS! I STILL THINK WE OUGHTA--
GREMLINS OR BABIES-- IT DON'T MATTER MUCH NOW. *WE DON'T HAVE A SHIP ANYMORE*, REMEMBER?
AS FOR THIS BUNCH OF DIRTY *KIDNAPPERS--!*
NO, DAD! THEY *DIDN'T REALIZE--*
YOU'RE ROX'S PARENTS? I GUESS WE OWE YOU AN EXPLANATION...AND AN APOLOGY.
BOOM!
POP!
GET BACK, EVERYBODY!
LOOKS LIKE SHE'S IN HER DEATH THROES, FELLAS.
BOOM!

AND HERE WE ARE--STUCK ON AN ASTEROID IN THE MIDDLE OF NOWHERE!
AND WE'RE FLAT BROKE NOW, TOO!
LOOKS LIKE RED MYK WAS RIGHT ABOUT US--TURNS OUT ***WE ARE*** BUMS!
BUMS--KIDNAPPERS--PIRATES--WHATEVER YOU ALL ARE...
...YOU LOOK LIKE YOU COULD USE A PLACE TO REST AND A HOT MEAL.
MOL, I DON'T WANT THESE--!
SURE YOU DO, J'OH! THESE FELLAS JUST BROUGHT YOUR DAUGHTER AND HER BEST FRIEND HOME...
WELL, YEAH. BUT--!
...AND WE'RE GONNA AT LEAST FEED THEM FOR THEIR TROUBLE!
...AND THEN ***I'D*** LIKE TO HEAR THE ***STORY*** THEY HAVE TO TELL!
NO USE TRYIN' TO CHANGE HER MIND WHEN YOU GET ***THAT*** LOOK!
C'MON, FELLAS.
HA! ***MY*** MOM!

...AND SO WE LIMPED BACK HERE! IF NOT FOR THESE TWO KIDS...
AND THE BABIES!
...AND THE BABIES, THAT QUARKCORP SHIP WOULDA BLOWN US TO ATOMS!
AMAZING!
THANK YOU ALL FOR SAVING ROX FROM RED MYK! AND FOR GETTING THE KIDS BACK HERE SAFE AND SOUND.
IF I EVER GET MY HANDS ON MYK AGAIN, I'LL-- *GRRRR!!!*

AND THERE'S STILL THE FACT THAT YOU GUYS ARE *PIRATES!* YOU'VE LOOTED SHIPS ALL ACROSS FAR RIM!
ONLY *QUARKCORP* SHIPS! WHAT WE DID WAS *PAYBACK* FOR STEALIN' OUR LIVELIHOODS!
WELL, I CAN SURE UNDERSTAND THAT.

THEIR WORMHOLE IS WHY I ENDED UP OUT OF A JOB, TRYIN' TO SCRAPE TOGETHER A LIVING FOR MY FAMILY WITH THIS SORRY SALVAGE YARD.

YOU KNOW,
MAYBE WE RAN AWAY FROM THE PROBLEM, INSTEAD OF FACING IT DOWN LIKE YOU GUYS.
WE FACED 'EM DOWN ALL RIGHT-- AND LOOK WHERE IT GOT US!

BOY, ALL THIS TROUBLE OVER SOMETHING AS ***UNSTABLE*** AS A WORMHOLE!
WHAT DO YOU MEAN "UNSTABLE"?

WORMHOLES ARE SUPER UNSTABLE. THEY BLINK IN AND OUT OF EXISTENCE ALL THE TIME.
I'VE BEEN READING UP ON THOSE THINGS.
OF COURSE YOU HAVE.

SO HOW COME QUARK'S GATE IS STILL AROUND?
I SUPPOSE THE QUARKCORP ENGINEERS FOUND SOME WAY TO --Y'KNOW--STABILIZE IT.
THEY COULD DO THAT?!
THEY MUST'VE. THAT HOLE'S BEEN AROUND FOR A WHILE NOW.

ZAM, DOES THAT MEAN IT COULD BE... *UNSTABILIZED?*
I SUPPOSE SO. I'D HAVE TO DO THE MATH ON IT, BUT IT SEEMS LOGICAL.

WHAT'S EVERYBODY LOOKIN' AT?

MOM, ZAM'S GONNA NEED TO USE THE SHOP COMPUTER.

FELLAS, WE'RE ***NOT RETIRING*** FROM THE ***PIRATE*** BUSINESS JUST YET!
ZZZ
?!?

IN THE CYCLES THAT FOLLOW...
DO YOU REALLY THINK THERE'S A WAY TO DO THIS?
THAT'S WHAT THEY'RE TRYIN' TO FIGURE OUT IN THERE...
ZAM'S RIGHT... IN *THEORY*, ANYWAY!
IT'S GOTTA BE THOSE RINGS THEY BUILT THAT ARE STABILIZING THE THING.
QUARKCORP.CO
WORMHOLES
WE'LL NEED AT LEAST A MILLION GIGAWATTS TO PULL THIS OFF.
WHERE CAN WE GET THAT KIND OF POWER?!
...A CURIOUS CREW WAITS FOR NEWS...
Far Rim SALVAGE & REPAIR
ZAM TOLD ME YESTERDAY THEY WERE GETTIN' CLOSE.
CLOSE TO *WHAT?* ALL THAT MATH IS WAY OVER MY HEAD.
WE'VE BEEN CRUNCHING THE NUMBERS.
THERE IS *ONE SOURCE* FOR THE KIND OF POWER WE'LL NEED.
HMM...
IT *SEEMS* TO MAKE SENSE.
SO YOU THINK IT'LL WORK, ZAM?

UM... PROBABLY.
SHE MEANS "YES"!
LET'S FILL IN THE CREW.
FINALLY-- HERE THEY COME!
SO, DID YOU FOLKS FIGURE IT OUT?
GUYS...
...WE'VE ALL GOT A LOT OF WORK TO DO.
WOO HOO! THE QUASAR TORRENT FLIES AGAIN!
...WE HOPE.
DO YOU REALLY THINK WE CAN SALVAGE THE OLD GIRL?
SHE WON'T BE AS GOOD AS NEW, BUT WE'VE GOT ENOUGH PARTS AROUND HERE TO GET HER SPACE-BORNE AGAIN.
?!?!?
JUST FOLLOW TILDA'S LEAD. SHE'S A WHIZ AT WIRING.
WE'LL NEED AT LEAST A DOZEN SINGLE-PILOT RIGS. DO YOU HAVE THAT MANY WE CAN GET UP AND RUNNING?
I THINK SO.

HOW'S IT COMIN', SPECS?
NOT BAD, BUT I'M NOT SURE I LIKE TAKIN' ORDERS FROM THIS *RUNT!*
MRMMM!
PULL THOSE OLD FRAMISTATS, BUGS. THEY SHOULD FIT THE *TORRENT* JUST FINE.
I FOUND THOSE BOOSTERS YA WANTED.
NICE! TAKE 'EM TO THE GARAGE.
THESE PUPS SURE KNOW THIS SHIP INSIDE OUT!
THEY OUGHT TO-- IT'S THE ONLY HOME THEY'VE EVER HAD!
SQUIGGY, OLD BUDDY!
LOOK WHAT I FOUND CLEANIN' OUT THE EXHAUST!

AWWW! LOOK AT AXYL AND HIS NEW PAL!
SHH! DON'T WAKE 'EM. THEY WAS UP ALL NIGHT WORKIN' ON THAT OLD SHUTTLE'S ENGINE.
Z Z Z
I DON'T TAKE ORDERS FROM NO PUP!
BETTER LISTEN TO HIM, SPYK! THAT PUP KNOWS MORE ABOUT POWER CELLS THAN YOU AND I EVER WILL!
HOW MANY RIGS DO WE HAVE RUNNING NOW?
EIGHT. WE'LL NEED A FEW MORE.
WE GOT THOSE SYNCHRONIZERS WORKIN' PERFECT, ZAM!
GREAT JOB, GUYS!
A COUPLE MORE CYCLES AND WE SHOULD BE READY.
THEN COMES THE SCARY PART.

SCARY! HA! REMEMBER--OUR GUYS ARE PIRATES! THEY'VE GOT NERVES OF STEEL!
THEY'RE NOT WHAT I'M WORRIED ABOUT.

I DON'T LIKE YOU GIRLS BEING INVOLVED IN THE DANGEROUS PART OF THIS PLAN!
I DON'T LIKE IT MUCH EITHER, BUT THEY'RE THE ONLY ONES WHO CAN DO IT!
WE'LL BE FINE, MOM!

AND I'M GOING ALONG, TOO, SO I'LL MAKE SURE THEY STAY SAFE.
WHO KEEPS YOU SAFE? I DON'T WANT TO LOSE ROX OR ZAM... OR YOU!

NOBODY'S LOSING ANYBODY! WE'VE GOT THIS ALL FIGURED OUT! RIGHT, ZAM?
I'VE RECHECKED ALL THE CALCULATIONS. IT SHOULD WORK FINE.

NOBODY'S DYIN'! THIS IS ABOUT LIVING! TOMORROW WE'RE TAKING BACK WHAT'S OURS...

...WITH A HIDDY HIDDY...

YO!

YO!

YO!

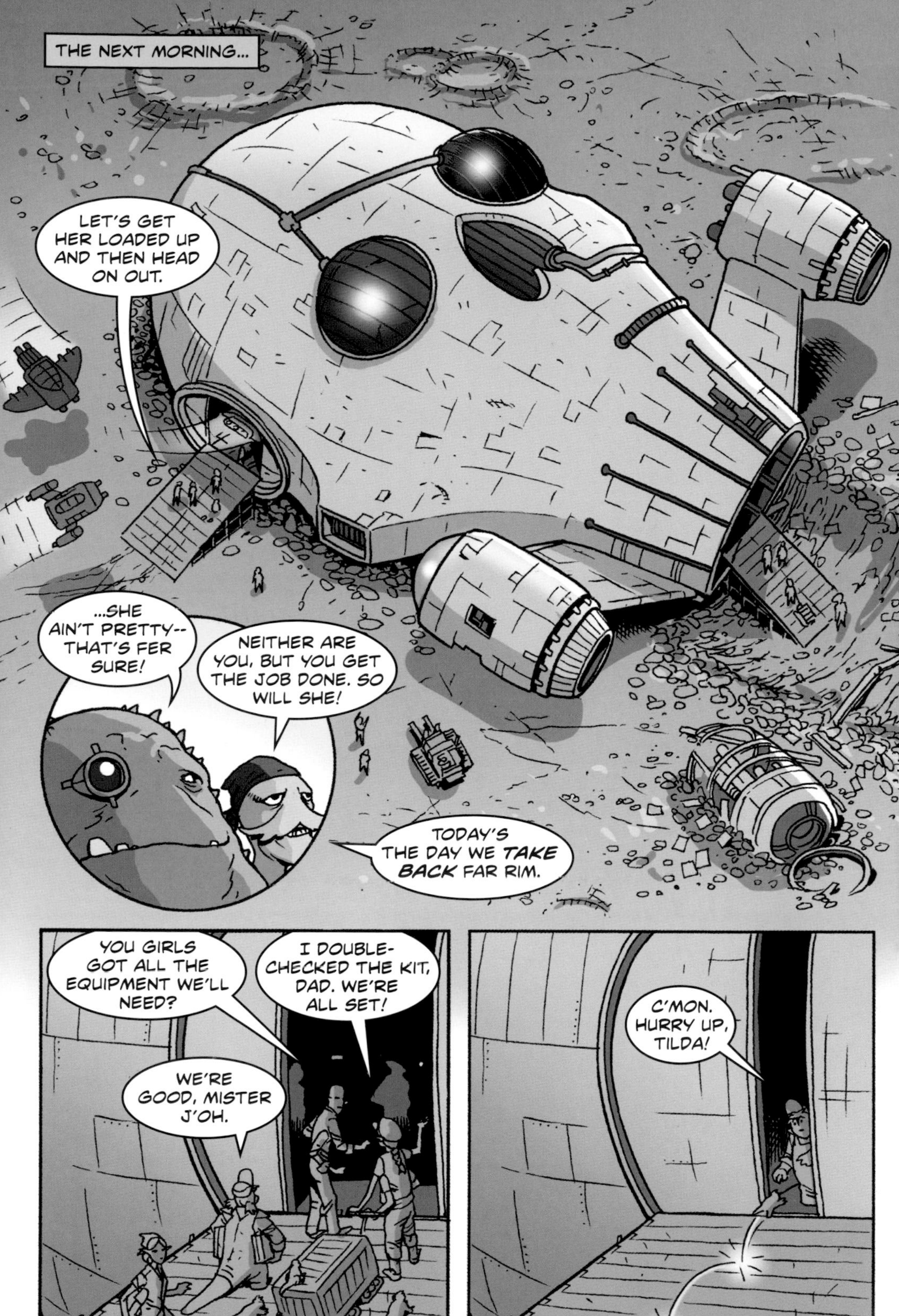
THE NEXT MORNING...
LET'S GET HER LOADED UP AND THEN HEAD ON OUT.
...SHE AIN'T PRETTY-- THAT'S FER SURE!
NEITHER ARE YOU, BUT YOU GET THE JOB DONE. SO WILL SHE!
TODAY'S THE DAY WE TAKE BACK FAR RIM.
YOU GIRLS GOT ALL THE EQUIPMENT WE'LL NEED?
I DOUBLE-CHECKED THE KIT, DAD. WE'RE ALL SET!
WE'RE GOOD, MISTER J'OH.
C'MON. HURRY UP, TILDA!

ALL SYSTEMS ARE GO.
CARGO BAY IS SECURE.
LET'S FIRE IT UP, FELLAS!
YAHOOO!!!
BBROOOOM
WE DID IT, FELLAS!
THE QUASAR TORRENT IS BACK!

BANG
...MORE OR LESS.
POP

ARE THE PUPS FILLED IN ON WHAT WE'RE GOING TO DO, ZAM?
I'VE BEEN TEACHING THEM TRACTOR BEAM THEORY.

HOW DO YOU KNOW THE *NEUTRON STORM* EVEN ***HAS*** A TRACTOR BEAM? THEY ***NEVER*** USED ONE ON THE *TORRENT*!
'CAUSE THEY WEREN'T TRYING TO CAPTURE US...
...THEY WANTED TO ***BLOW US UP!***

I GUARANTEE THAT A MODERN SHIP LIKE THE *NEUTRON STORM* HAS A TRACTOR BEAM ON BOARD...
...AND IT'LL BE A ***BIG ONE!***

YOU FELLAS HAVE THE ***DANGEROUS*** PART OF THIS JOB.
YOU MEAN THE ***FUN*** PART!
YOU GUYS TAKE CARE OF YOURSELVES.

THE GIRLS AND I WILL HANDLE ***THE REST...***

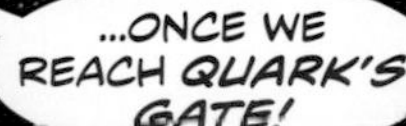
...ONCE WE REACH ***QUARK'S GATE!***

SOME CYCLES LATER...
THIS IS IT! QUARK'S GATE--DEAD AHEAD!
AND THERE'S THE NEUTRON STORM, PATROLIN' THE PERIMETER, JUST LIKE WE EXPECTED!
BATTLE STATIONS, EVERYBODY!

C'MON, AWAY TEAM--
LET'S GET TO OUR SHIPS!
IT'S GO-TIME!

NAVIGATION, READY!

ENGINE ROOM, READY!

FLIGHT DECK, READY!

BRIDGE, READY!

SHIELDS AND DEFENSE SYSTEMS, READY!

WEAPONS, READY!

INFILTRATION TEAM, READY!
YOU BE CAREFUL!
I'LL MAKE SURE THEY STAY SAFE, MOL!

MEANWHILE...
JUST WHEN ARE YOUR BOSSES GONNA COME UP WITH THE CASH YOU OWE ME, WHISKERS?
THERE ARE PROPER CHANNELS FOR THIS SORT OF THING. YOUR REWARD FEE WILL BE AUTHORIZED AS SOON AS THE QUARKCORP BOARD MEETS THIS--
PARDON ME, COMMANDER--!

I'VE PICKED UP A FAST-APPROACHING VESSEL.
FROM IT'S ENERGY SIGNATURE, IT APPEARS TO BE...

...THE QUASAR TORRENT!
OR AT LEAST, WHAT'S LEFT OF HER!
WHAT?!

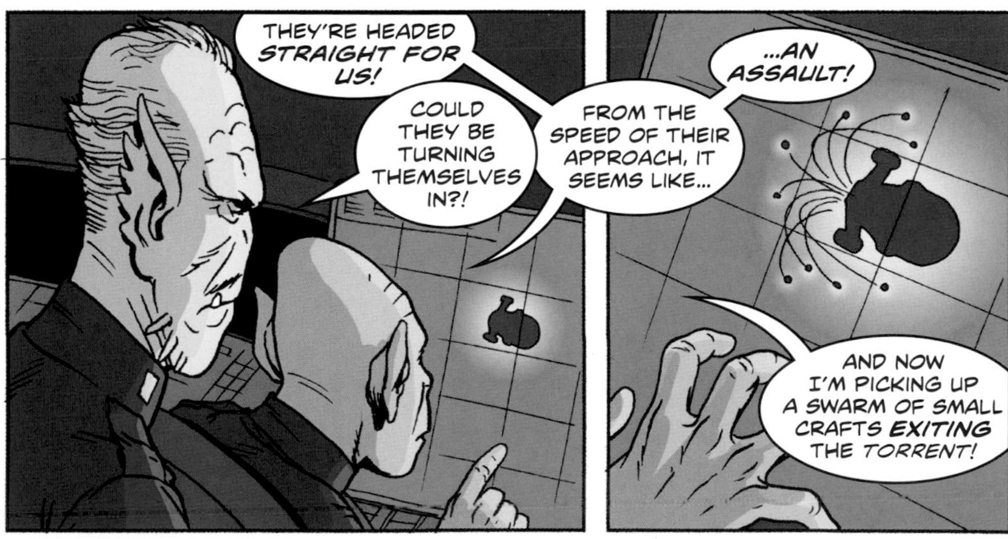
THEY'RE HEADED STRAIGHT FOR US!
COULD THEY BE TURNING THEMSELVES IN?!
FROM THE SPEED OF THEIR APPROACH, IT SEEMS LIKE...
...AN ASSAULT!
AND NOW I'M PICKING UP A SWARM OF SMALL CRAFTS EXITING THE TORRENT!

LET'S GET 'EM, GUYS!
YAH-HOOO!

AWAY TEAM TO BRIDGE-- OPERATION GIANT SLAYER IS A GO!
ATTACK!

ZAP!
ZAP!
HOW ABSURD! THOSE TINY CRAFTS CAN'T DESTROY A SHIP THIS SIZE!
THEY'RE SO SMALL, THEY'LL BE HARD TO SHOOT DOWN, SIR!
ZAP!
ZAP!
ZAP!
ZAP!
ZAP!

THEN LET'S TRAIN OUR LASER CANNONS ON THE QUASAR TORRENT!
INSTRUCT THE GUNNERY TEAM TO FIRE AT WILL!

ZRRT!
ZRRT!
ZRRT!
IT'S FLYING EVERY WHICH WAY, SIR! WE CAN'T GET A BEAD ON THEIR PATH!

THE BRIDGE SAYS THE TRAJECTORY RANDOMIZER YOU INSTALLED IS WORKIN' GREAT, J'OH! THEY CAN'T TARGET US!
NOW IT'S UP TO US!

LET'S HUSTLE, GIRLS! WE'VE GOT TO--

BOOM!
WHAT WAS *THAT?!*

OH NO! WE BLEW A CONVERTER ON ENGINE TWO! IT'LL BURN OUT IN NO TIME!
SPUT!
SPUT!
WE NEED A MECHANIC OVER THERE *RIGHT NOW!*

DANG! I'LL HAVE TO GO HOOK UP A BYPASS CIRCUIT!
WHAT ABOUT OUR *MISSION?!*

THE *TORRENT'S* AN EASY TARGET IF THAT ENGINE GOES OFFLINE! WE'LL HAVE TO DELAY OUR DEPARTURE UNTIL IT'S FIXED!
WITH LUCK, I'LL BE BACK IN A FEW MILLICYCLES.

YOU TWO WAIT RIGHT HERE! THIS'LL BE A QUICK FIX!
BUT--! BUT--!

ZAM, WE CAN'T DELAY THIS MISSION! EVERYTHING DEPENDS ON IT!!!
GULP! I-I THINK YOU'RE RIGHT, ROX!

THIS IS J'OH, FELLAS! I'M HEADED FOR ENGINE TWO! I THINK I CAN--
UH OH! THAT'S BAD!

WHAT'S BAD?!?!
UM--THE INFILTRATION TEAM SHUTTLE JUST TOOK OFF...
WITHOUT ME!!!
ER... I-I GUESS SO.

THOSE DUMB KIDS!!!
OOOOKAY. THIS'LL BE *EASY!*
I WOULDN'T SAY "*EASY*"...
WE CAN DO THIS! WITH THE OTHERS DISTRACTING THE *NEUTRON STORM* WITH THEIR ATTACK...
...WE JUST SNEAK AROUND TO HER UNDERSIDE, NICE AND QUIET!
CLINK!

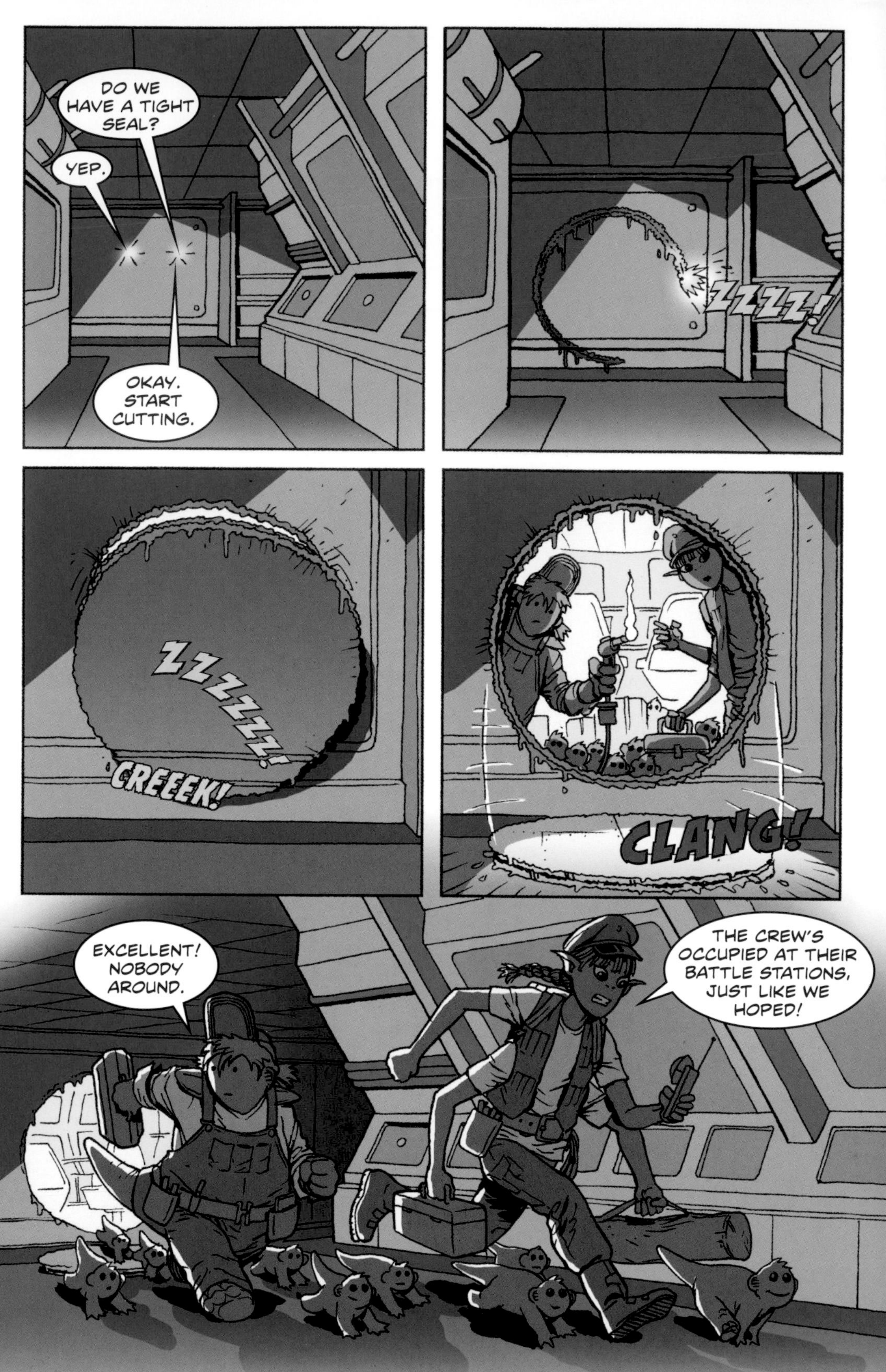

DO WE HAVE A TIGHT SEAL?
YEP.
OKAY. START CUTTING.
ZZZZZ!
ZZZZZZZ!
CREEEK!
CLANG!
EXCELLENT! NOBODY AROUND.
THE CREW'S OCCUPIED AT THEIR BATTLE STATIONS, JUST LIKE WE HOPED!

POWER READINGS SHOW IT'S THROUGH THIS HATCH.

WHOA!

GULP!
NOW *THAT'S* A TRACTOR BEAM!

BABIES, YOU KNOW WHAT TO DO! LET'S GET TO WORK-- *FAST!!!*
WE CAN DO THIS!
WE CAN DO THIS!

THE TORRENT CAN'T HOPE TO WIN! IT AIN'T LIKE MY GUYS TO DO SOMETHIN' THIS DUMB!
SHOOT THEM DOWN!
IT'S HARD, SIR! THEY'RE SMALL AND NIMBLE!

COMMANDER, I'M PICKING UP A POWER FLUCTUATION FROM OUR TRACTOR BEAM DRIVERS.
TRACTOR BEAM--! WHO CARES?! WE'RE IN THE MIDDLE OF A BATTLE!
???
ALERT!

WELL, YOU GUYS GOT YOUR HANDS FULL. I'M OFF TO MY CABIN.
GRRR! SOMEONE HIT SOME-THING!

OKAY, I'VE GOT THE POLARITY ROUTER INVERTED!
WE'RE ALMOST DONE WITH THESE NEW CONNECTIONS, TOO!

JEEZ! THIS WAS EASIER THAN I THOUGHT!

YEAH! WHO NEEDS ADULT SUPER-VISION?!

WELL, IF IT AIN'T MY OLD WRENCH-BENDERS!

!!!!!

I HEARD THERE WAS TROUBLE WITH THE TRACTOR BEAM DOWN HERE, AND I SAID TO MYSELF...

...NOW WHO DO I KNOW THAT JUST *LOVES* TINKERIN' WITH TRACTOR BEAMS?

RIGHT AWAY I THOUGHT OF *YOU TWO!*

WE GOT SOME UNFINISHED BUSINESS, YOU GIRLS AND ME...
...BUT I THINK WE CAN TAKE CARE 'A THAT *RIGHT HERE AND NOW!*
GRRRRRRRR!!!
WHA--?!
NOT *YOU GUYS* AGAIN!
RAWRRR!!!
GET 'IM, BABIES!!!

Y'KNOW, MYK, WE'D LOVE TO CHAT, BUT--
KLONK!
OWWW!
YEAH! SORRY, GOTTA RUN!
BONK!

GAAH!
LET'S GO, ZAM!

LEAVE THE TOOLS! TAKE THE BABIES!
C'MON, KIDS!
FWEET!

ALL ABOARD!
BOING!
BOING!
BOING!

GAAHH!! VICIOUS LITTLE SPACE RATS!
BOING!

C'MON! HURRY! HURRY!
GOOD JOB, BABIES!
BOING!
BOING!
BOING!

NO WAY! YOU TWO AIN'T GETTIN' AWAY THAT EASY!
WHERE'S MY BLASTER?!

S'LONG, MYK! LOOKS LIKE YOU'RE THE ONE THAT NEEDS A SPACESUIT THIS TIME!

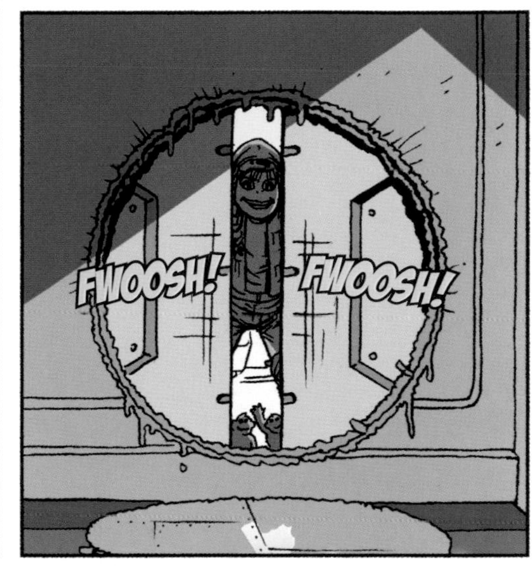
FWOOSH!
FWOOSH!

POP!
POP!
KA-CLANK
POP!
POP!

VROOSH!

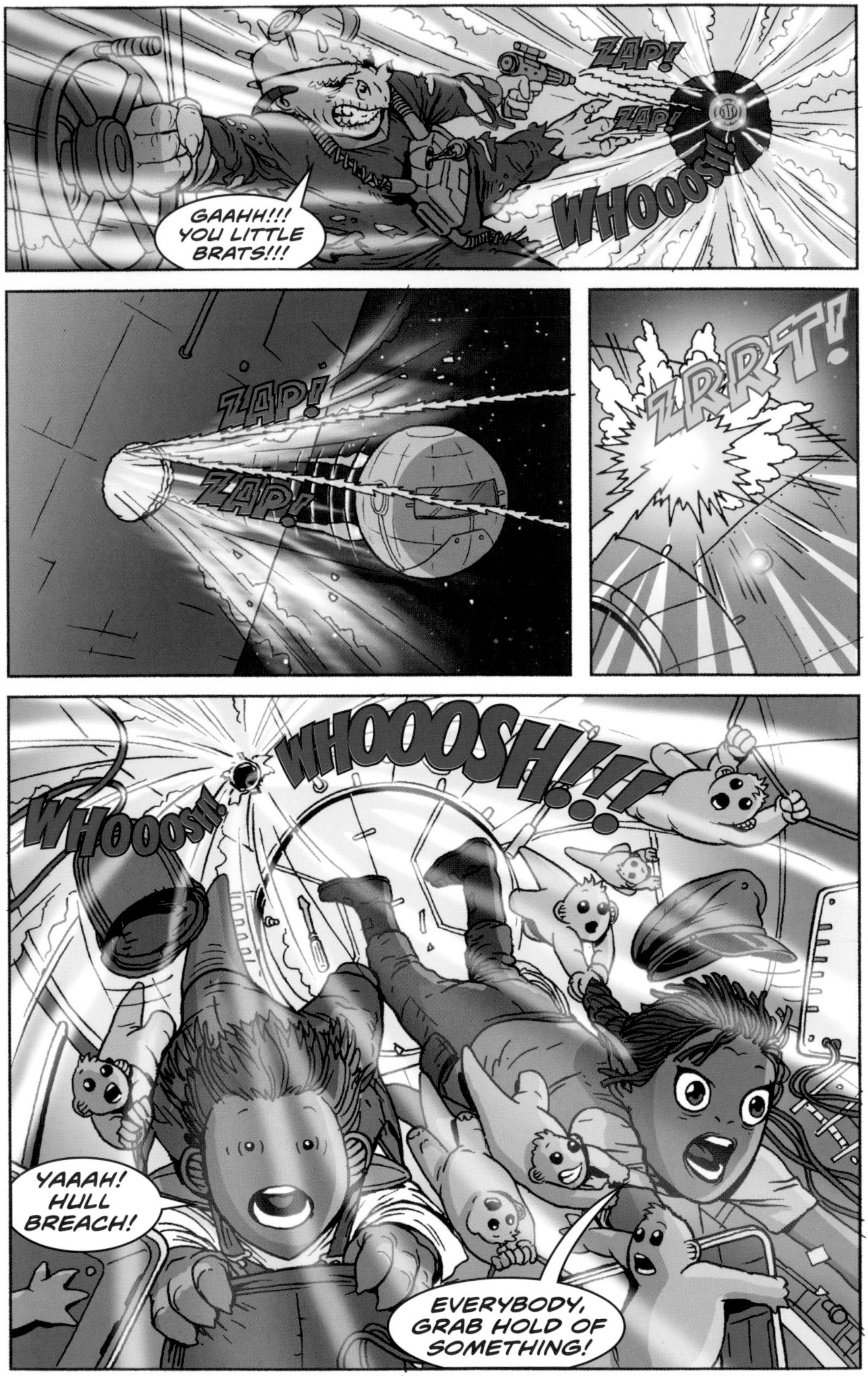

WHOOOSH!
WHOOOSH!!!
YAAAH! HULL BREACH!
EVERYBODY, GRAB HOLD OF SOMETHING!

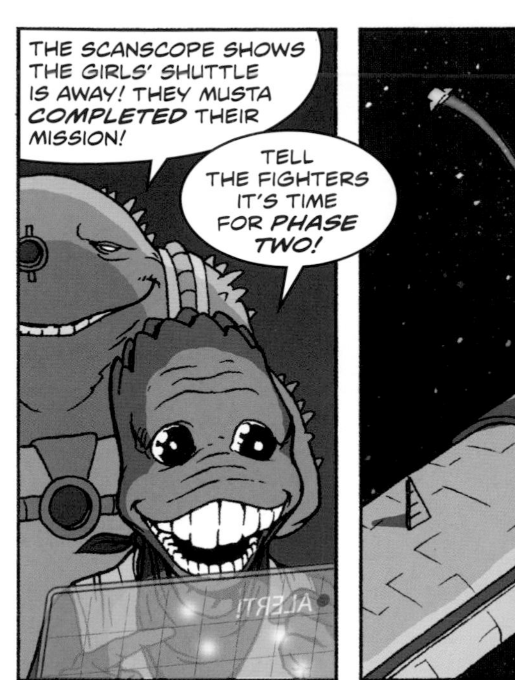
THE SCANSCOPE SHOWS THE GIRLS' SHUTTLE IS AWAY! THEY MUSTA COMPLETED THEIR MISSION!
TELL THE FIGHTERS IT'S TIME FOR PHASE TWO!
ALERT!

COMMANDER, THE ENEMY IS RETREATING IN ALL DIFFERENT DIRECTIONS!
COWARDS! THEY WON'T GET AWAY THAT EASILY!

WE'LL DRAW THEM ALL BACK! PREPARE THE TRACTOR BEAM!
AYE, SIR!

JEEZ! I BARELY GOT THAT HATCH SEALED OFF IN TIME!
RRRRRRR
HEY! THAT SOUNDS LIKE...

...THE TRACTOR BEAM! I BET THOSE KIDS SABOTAGED IT...
...AND THOSE DOPES ON THE BRIDGE ARE ABOUT TO TURN IT ON!
RRRRRRR

IT'S GONNA BLOW!
HHHMMMM

???
THAT'S FUNNY.
MMMMMMMMMMMMMMMMMMMMM
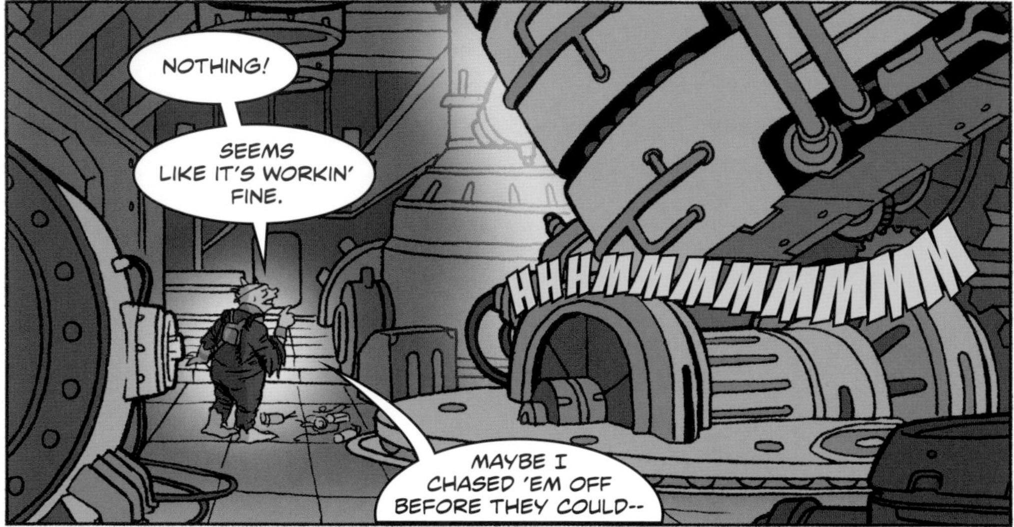
NOTHING!
SEEMS LIKE IT'S WORKIN' FINE.
HHHMMMMMMMMMMM
MAYBE I CHASED 'EM OFF BEFORE THEY COULD--

HEY! THOSE CABLES HAVE BEEN SWITCHED!

OH NO.

...AND THOSE LOOK LIKE POWER DAMPERS!

IS THERE A PROBLEM, ENSIGN?
SOMETHING'S NOT RIGHT, SIR! THE ENEMY IS GETTING FARTHER AWAY!

W-WE'RE REPELLING THEM!!!
...AND THE TRACTOR BEAM'S POWER LEVELS ARE GOING OFF THE SCALE!

TURN IT OFF, YOU FOOL!
I-I CAN'T!!!

WE'RE REPELLING INTO THE GATE!!!
IT'S WORKIN'!
OUR ATTACK MANUEVERED 'EM RIGHT INTO POSITION!
THIS IS GREAT!
LIKE WATER DOWN A DRAIN!

WOO HOO!
BUT HOW ARE THE GIRLS?!?
REPORT, ENSIGN!
THE WAY THE POWER'S BUILDING, AND GIVEN OUR TRAJECTORY...

SHUT DOWN THE TRACTOR BEAM! SHUT IT DOWN!!!
I-I CAN'T, SIR!!!

YAHOOOO!!!!
IT WORKED!
ERK!
WE POSITIONED THE NEUTRON STORM PERFECT TO REPEL ITSELF INTO THE WORMHOLE!
THE GIRLS DID IT, MOL!
YEP! AND ONCE ITS TRACTOR BEAM WRECKED THE RINGS, QUARK'S GATE BLINKED RIGHT OUT OF EXISTENCE!

ALL AWAY SHIPS, RETURN TO THE TORRENT!

WHAT DO YOU HEAR FROM THE GIRLS, AXYL?
UM...WELL... ALL VESSELS HAVE CHECKED IN...

...EXCEPT FOR ONE!

WHOOOOSH!!!!

HOLD ON, ROX! HOLD ON, BABIES!

WE CAN'T HOLD ON FOR-EVER!

ONCE THE OXY TANKS ARE EMPTY, THE PULLING WILL STOP...
...BUT THEN WE'LL SUFFOCATE!
...IF THE BABIES CAN HOLD ON THAT LONG!
WE'VE GOTTA FIND A WAY TO SEAL THAT HOLE!
OKAY...
...I-I KNOW WHAT I GOTTA DO!
ZAM! WHAT ARE YOU GOING TO--?!?

ZAM-
NO!!!...
WHOOOOOSH!!!...
I'M GONNA HATE THIS!

HUF! HUF!
THIS IS SO UNDIGNIFIED.
hssssss
!!!

HUF! HUF!
ZAM-- YOU ARE THE *GREATEST, BRAVEST, BESTEST*--!
hssssss
HUF! HUF!
LET'S DISCUSS THIS LATER--

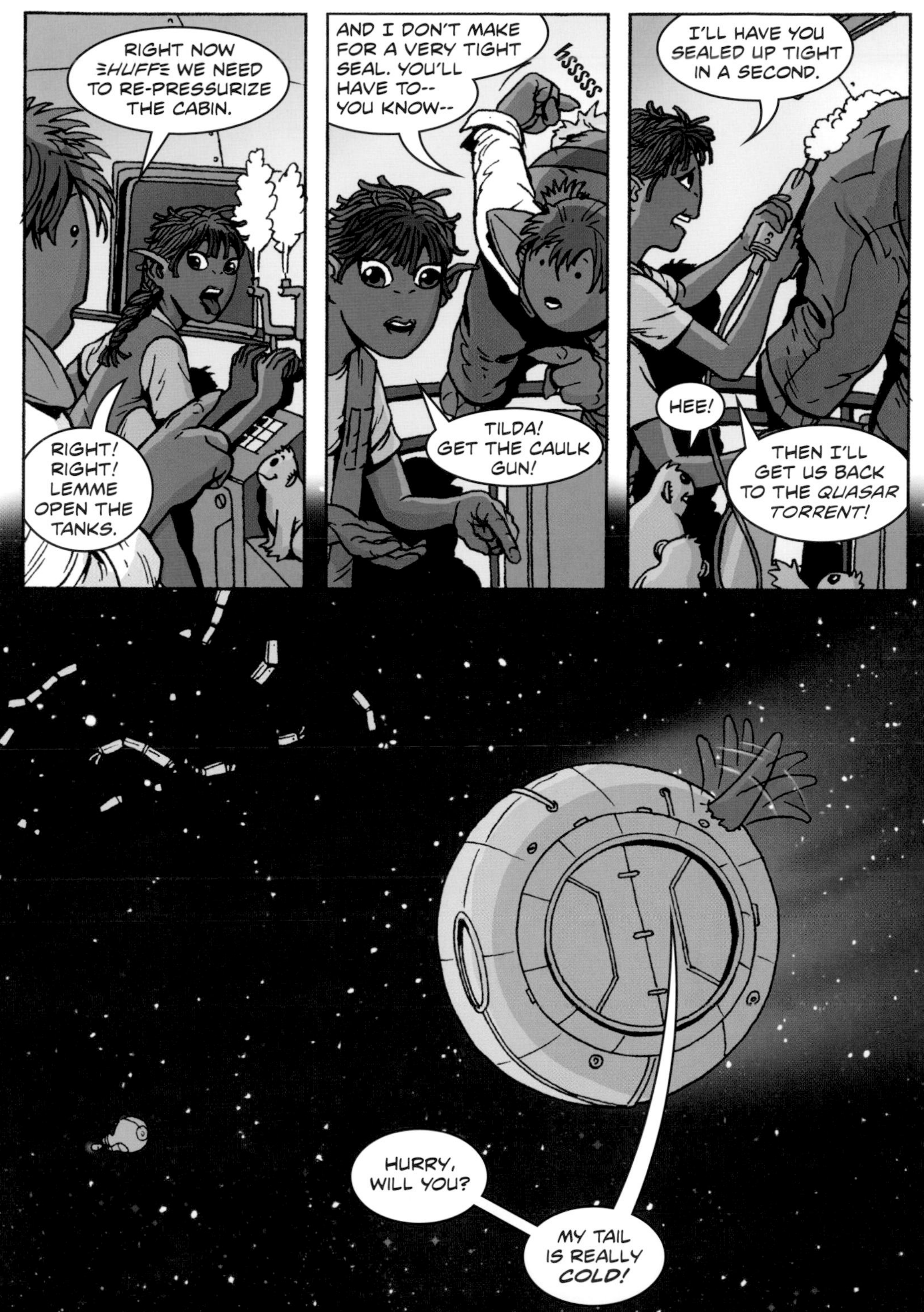
RIGHT NOW
=HUFF= WE NEED
TO RE-PRESSURIZE
THE CABIN.
RIGHT!
RIGHT!
LEMME
OPEN THE
TANKS.
AND I DON'T MAKE
FOR A VERY TIGHT
SEAL. YOU'LL
HAVE TO--
YOU KNOW--
hssssss
TILDA!
GET THE CAULK
GUN!
I'LL HAVE YOU
SEALED UP TIGHT
IN A SECOND.
HEE!
THEN I'LL
GET US BACK
TO THE QUASAR
TORRENT!
HURRY,
WILL YOU?
MY TAIL
IS REALLY
COLD!

CHAPTER 8

ROX, WE'RE SUPPOSED TO HAVE THAT STARLINER COMING IN FOR MAINTENANCE TODAY. ARE WE READY FOR IT?
SURE, DAD. STACHE AND FYNN HAVE THE LANDING CRATER ALL PREPPED AND READY.

THE SCHEDULE SAYS CRUSTY'S GONNA DROP BY ON HIS RUN TO KESSLE!
YEAH. HE'S PICKIN' UP SUPPLIES FOR THE DINER HE AND GIL ARE STARTING ON THE MOON STATION.
YIKES! I'M NOT SURE *THAT'S* A GOOD IDEA! I TASTED GIL'S COOKING WHEN I WAS ON BOARD THE *TORRENT!*

EVEN BANDERSLATH CASSEROLE IS BETTER THAN--
HEY! THERE'S *SPYK'S* NEW RIG COMIN' IN! LET'S HAIL HIM ON THE COMLINK.

HI, FOLKS! GOT ROOM FOR A COUPLE A' SPACE TRAMPS?
NOPE. BUT WE'RE ALWAYS HAPPY TO SEE OLD FRIENDS.
SET 'ER DOWN ON CRATER FOUR, FELLAS.

SALVAGE & REPAIR
SPYK! PATCH!
ROX! ARE YOU GETTIN' *TALLER?!*
HI, FOLKS!

YOU HEARD ABOUT GIL AND CRUSTY'S DINER...

...BUGS IS NAVIGATOR ON A SPACE FREIGHTER...

...SPECS IS A FOREMAN ON THAT NEW SPACE STATION OUT BY SIRIUS...

...AND AXYL-- HE OPENED A FLOWER SHOP ON EDEN THREE!

I IMAGINE WE'LL ALL GET ON FINE, SO LONG AS QUARKCORP DOESN'T COME AROUND TO STIR UP TROUBLE AGAIN!

I THINK WE'RE SAFE THERE. FROM WHAT I HEARD...

...THE *NEUTRON STORM* ENDED UP ON THE OTHER SIDE OF THE COLLAPSED WORMHOLE NEAR QUARKCORP'S HOME WORLD!

THE SUITS BUSTED THAT COMMANDER FOR LETTIN' QUARK'S GATE COLLAPSE...

YOU'RE FIRED!

SAD!

...AND RED MYK NEVER DID GET HIS BLOOD MONEY!

BUT WE HAD A **DEAL!**

QUARKCORP IS ALL ABOUT THE BOTTOM LINE. WITH QUARK'S GATE GONE THEY GOT NO REASON TO COME AROUND FAR RIM ANYMORE.

HEY, WHERE'S ZAM!

WHERE DO YOU THINK? IN THE SHOP TINKERING WITH HER CREW, OF COURSE!

HOLD THAT THING STEADY, TILDA!

HO-KAY!

PEG, IS THAT POWER CELL CHARGED YET?

UM... PROLLY.

"*PROBABLY*"!

PROL-LA-LEE!

!!! WHAT KIND OF A SHIP IS *THIS?!*

AN EXPERIMENT ZAM AND I HAVE BEEN WORKIN' ON. WE'RE DESIGNING A *QUANTUM DRIVE RACER!*

THAT REMINDS ME, ROX--I'VE DRAWN UP SOME NEW PLANS I WANT YOU TO LOOK AT.

YOU KIDS LOOK AT YOUR PLANS. WE'RE GONNA GO TO THE HOUSE AND CATCH UP.
DO YOU GUYS LIKE BOROLLIAN ALE?
NOW YER TALKIN'!
NICE!

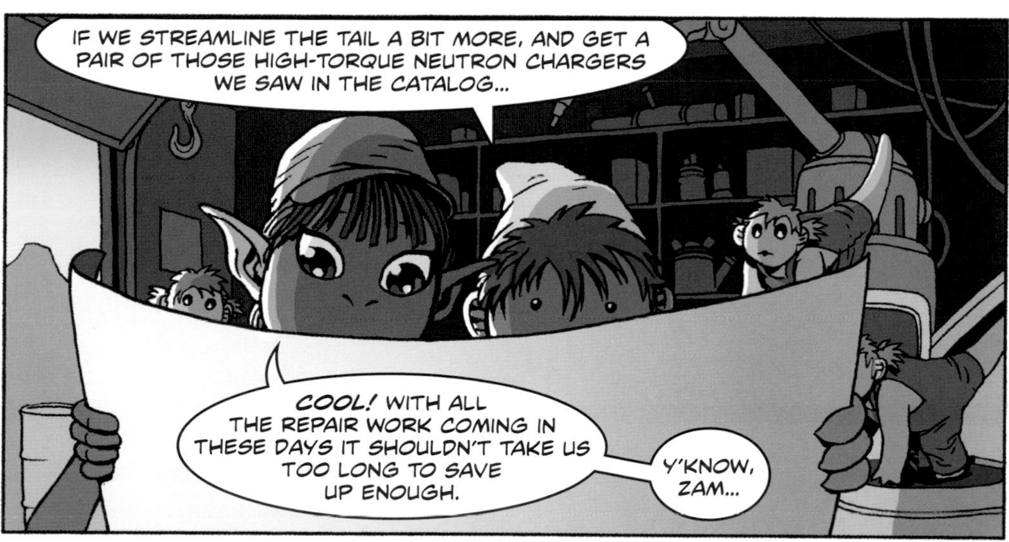

IF WE STREAMLINE THE TAIL A BIT MORE, AND GET A PAIR OF THOSE HIGH-TORQUE NEUTRON CHARGERS WE SAW IN THE CATALOG...
COOL! WITH ALL THE REPAIR WORK COMING IN THESE DAYS IT SHOULDN'T TAKE US TOO LONG TO SAVE UP ENOUGH.
Y'KNOW, ZAM...

...I THINK I LIKE BEIN' A SHIP DESIGNER EVEN MORE THAN BEIN' A PIRATE!
JEEZ! OF COURSE! BESIDES, YOU WERE NEVER REALLY A PIRATE!

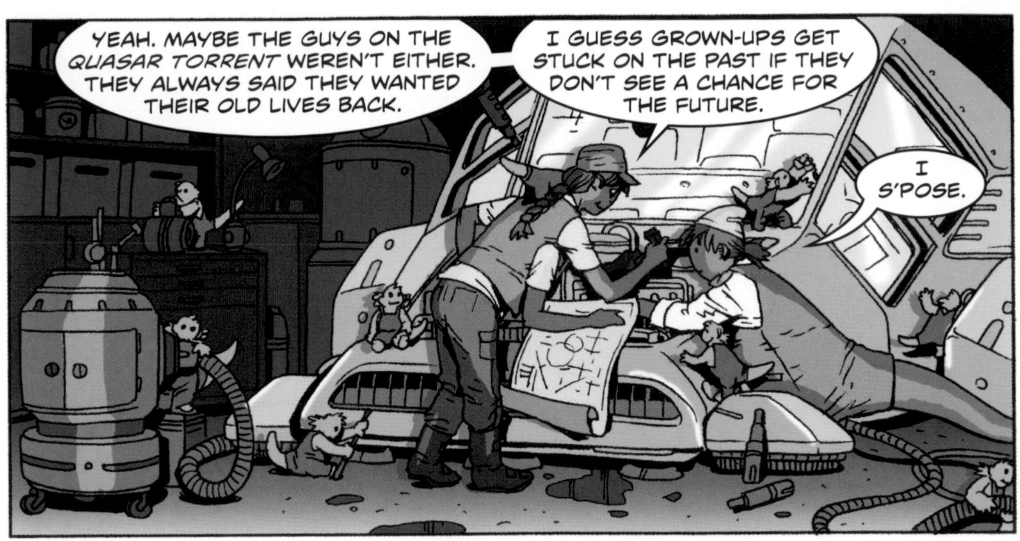
YEAH. MAYBE THE GUYS ON THE *QUASAR TORRENT* WEREN'T EITHER. THEY ALWAYS SAID THEY WANTED THEIR OLD LIVES BACK.
I GUESS GROWN-UPS GET STUCK ON THE PAST IF THEY DON'T SEE A CHANCE FOR THE FUTURE.
I S'POSE.

HAVE YOU THOUGHT ABOUT CHANGING THE INFLUX RATIO ON THE HYDROCARRIAGE TO MAKE...
...TO MAKE THE FUSION REACTOR MORE EFFICIENT? SURE! GOOD THINKIN', ROX!

Y'KNOW, WE'RE GETTING ***PRETTY*** GOOD AT THIS STUFF!
ONLY ***PRETTY*** GOOD?! YOU GOTTA HAVE CONFIDENCE, ZAM!
WHY, FOR A COUPLE OF ***GENIUSES*** LIKE US...

...THE SKY'S THE LIMIT!

Creating Quantum Mechanics

One of the things I like best about being a children's book author and illustrator is visiting schools to talk to kids about my work. During visits, I always get questions about how I create my artwork and stories. To help answer those questions for readers whose schools I'll never get to, here's a quick glimpse into how *Quantum Mechanics* went from an idea in my head to the book in your hands...

Quantum Mechanics: The Picture Book!

Quantum Mechanics started out years ago, not as a graphic novel, but as an idea for a children's picture book. Deciding what my next book project should be usually begins by imagining what would be the most fun to draw. The answer, at that moment, turned out to be aliens and spaceships. After rolling a few ideas around in my head, I came up with the idea of two humble alien mechanics who are kidnapped by intergalactic pirates and forced to repair the buccaneers' spaceship.

A picture book is a lot shorter than a graphic novel, so the story was simpler back then, plus the two heroes were a pair of adult males. But if you look at sketches and finished art for that project, you'll see the seeds of Rox and Zam's adventure.

I never got a publisher interested in the picture book. (That happens a lot to authors!) The characters and concepts sat gathering dust in my files for a while, but the idea of drawing aliens and spaceships still appealed to me a few years later as I hatched a new graphic novel project. No creative effort is ever wasted, and ideas can be recycled easier than plastic!

A few sketches and one finished illustration from the picture book proposal that eventually became Quantum Mechanics. *The shots of the* Quasar Torrent *shown here eventually made it into the graphic novel (see pages 23-25).*

Start to Finish: The Story Outline

Turning my picture book into a graphic novel meant there were a lot of changes to be made. The main characters became young girls, and the story had to expand from thirty-two pages to over two hundred! Here's a tip for creating a tale readers will connect with: All your key characters have to be working toward a goal, or maybe even several conflicting goals. Rox wants to go home...or maybe be a glamourous pirate. Zam wants to work on cool spaceships...or maybe be part of a family for the first time in her life. The pirates want their old lives back...or maybe to have a future. Those conflicting desires are the keys to interesting characters and an interesting story!

I always work out my story from beginning to end before I do any drawing. Making up a story as you draw is a surefire way to waste a lot of time and effort at the drawing board.

From Idea to Reality: Character Design

Once a story is well defined, the next step is to design all the characters, settings, and props. I do a lot of trial-and-error sketching to match the look of my characters to the personalities I've imagined. Fun fact: Rox and Zam are very loosely based on what I had read about Steve Jobs and Steve Wozniak, the co-founders of Apple Computer, Inc. Having these personalites in mind helped focus my thoughts on how they'd act and what they'd look like.

Here are some examples of how I think about character design: What attribute would an alien grease monkey find most useful? An extra set of hands! What form should the spaceship of lovable pirates take? A jolly roger with its tongue sticking out!

▲ *Early sketches of Zam, Rox, Mol, and J'oh. All will change a bit in their finished designs.*

▲ *Early sketches of a few supporting characters.*

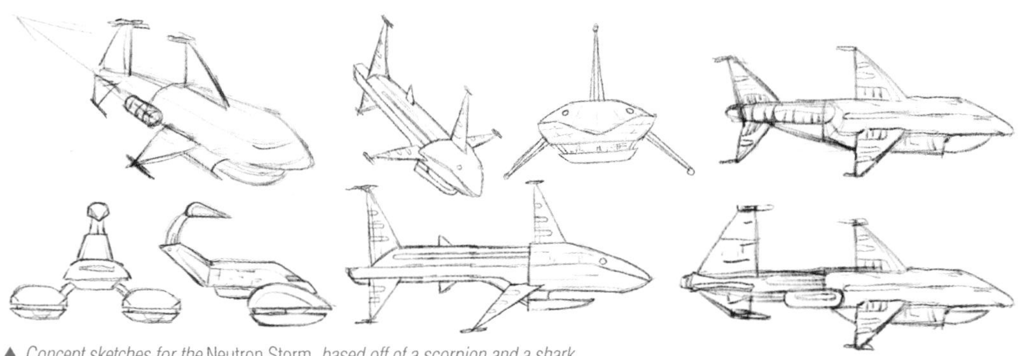

▲ *Concept sketches for the* Neutron Storm, *based off of a scorpion and a shark.*

▲ Rox and Zam model sheets. Once designs are nailed down, I like to make sure I know how to draw the characters' faces well enough that they can express any emotion they may need to show.

Deciding How to Tell Your Story: Thumbnail Sketches

Next comes the *real* work of a comic artist: deciding how my pictures will tell my story! What do I show? What *don't* I show? When do I use a close-up, or a faraway view, or something in-between? What angle do I show the action from? How many panels do I need for the events on a given page? What size are they, and how will they fit together?

Comic storytelling is complicated.

If I tried to make these decisions while drawing full-sized pages, I'd find myself constantly changing my mind and erasing. I save myself a ton of effort by planning page layouts first with a small, rough sketch called a "thumbnail sketch."

My thumbnail sketches are ugly and scribbly. You can barely tell what's going on in them—but I can. These sketches are only seen by me (and now you, of course); they only have to be detailed enough so that I know what to draw to tell my story clearly on the finished page. After a few minutes of scribbling and a few side notes to help me remember what story points to make, then I have a clear plan for a finished page. And it only takes a few minutes instead of a few hours!

I did a thumbnail sketch for every one of the 209 pages in *Quantum Mechanics* before I ever drew a single finished page. I made all my storytelling and pacing decisions in these scribbles. Doing thumbnails is like making sure you have a map to follow before you go on a long, long journey.

▲ *Actual-size thumbnail sketches for pages 186 and 187. I plan pairs of pages together, just the way you see them in the book. I think of two-page spreads the way a writer thinks of paragraphs—distinct pieces of a whole story.*

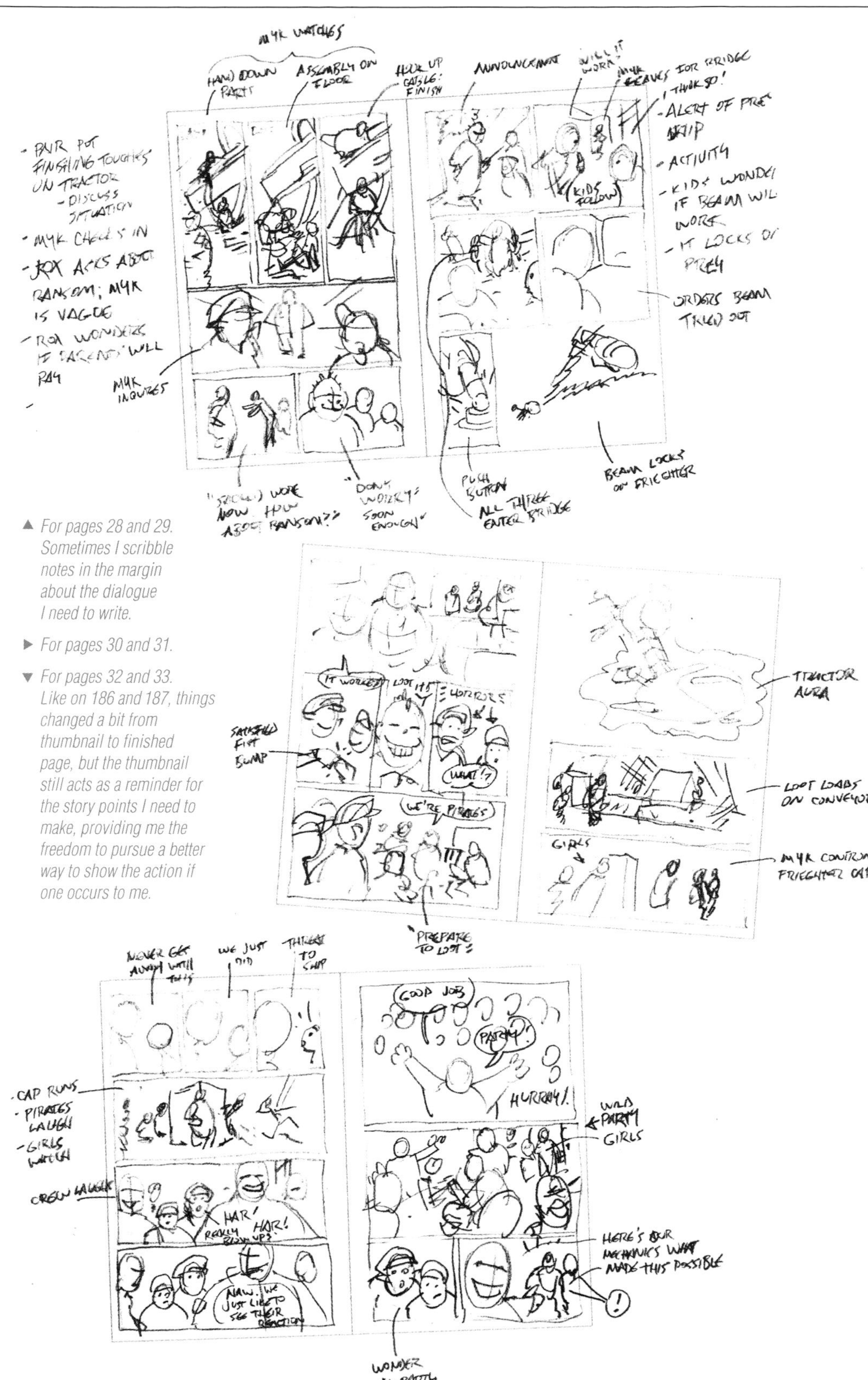

▲ For pages 28 and 29. Sometimes I scribble notes in the margin about the dialogue I need to write.

► For pages 30 and 31.

▼ For pages 32 and 33. Like on 186 and 187, things changed a bit from thumbnail to finished page, but the thumbnail still acts as a reminder for the story points I need to make, providing me the freedom to pursue a better way to show the action if one occurs to me.

Getting Your Story Down: Pencils

With thumbnails providing a clear plan for the storytelling and pace, the next step was to draw. The line art for *Quantum Mechanics* was done on 11" x 17" sheets of paper—much larger than the pages are printed—so I could add the detail I wanted without straining my eyes or my wits. Artists draw in pencil first so we can remove our mistakes with a few strokes of an eraser. I don't bother to include every detail in the pencilled art. Clarity and details will come in the inking stage, but the pencils are where I make sure my drawings are clear and well composed. Pencilling a page for *Quantum Mechanics* usually took two to three hours.

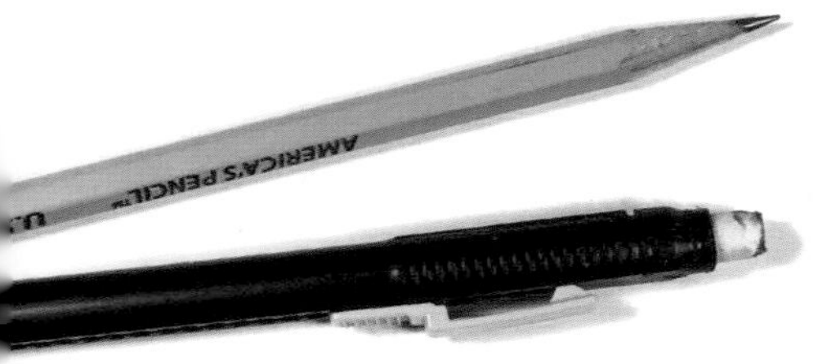

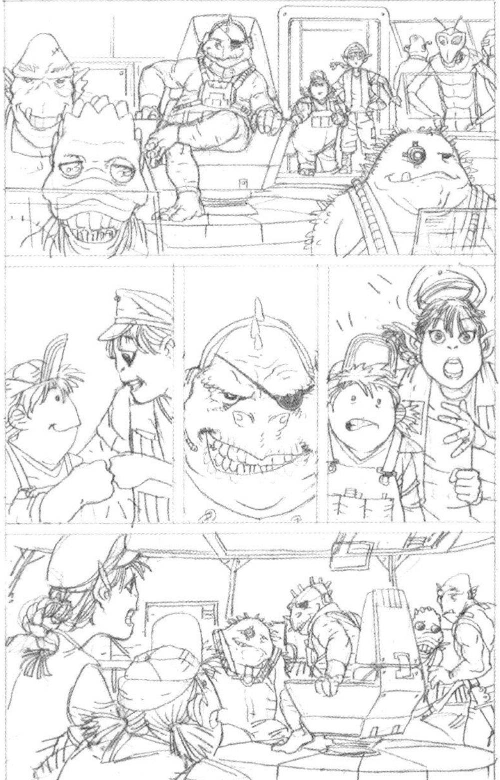

▶ *This shows a panel of pencil art at actual size. Note that I left space at the top for the word balloons to come— I try to avoid wasting my time drawing details that will get covered up by dialogue or captions.*

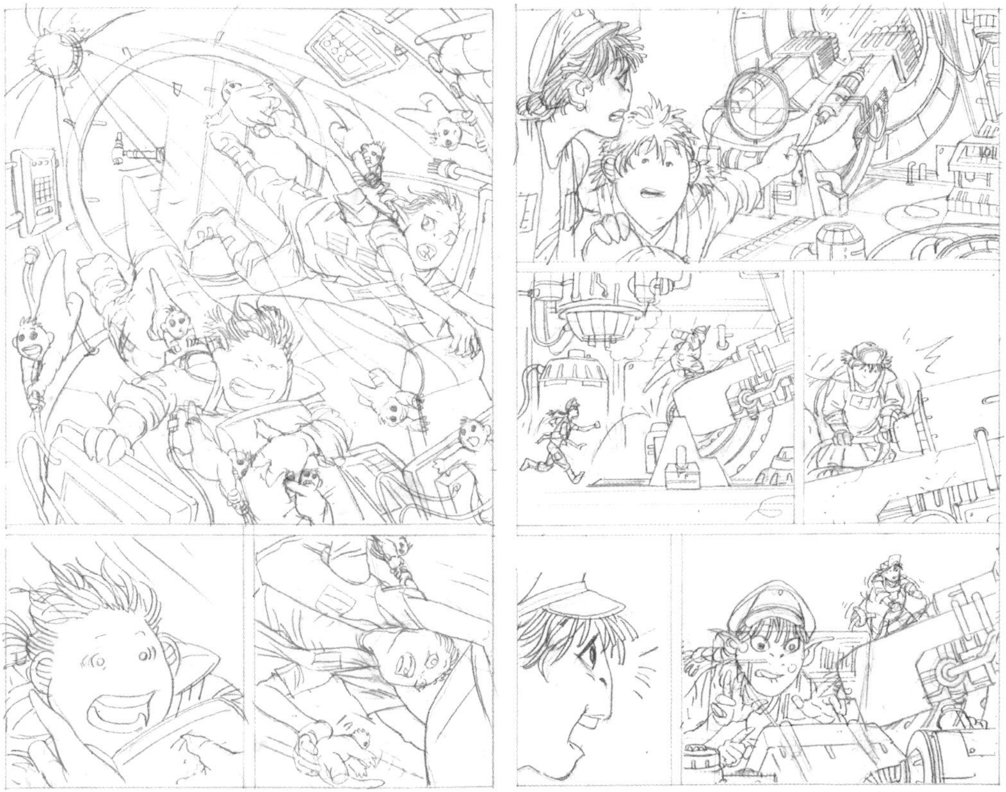

Giving Your Characters Their Say: Scripting and Lettering

Many comic authors write a full script, like one for a movie, before they ever do thumbnails or finished pencils. I approach writing dialogue a bit differently. I like to make sure my pictures do most of the storytelling, so I draw those first. Then I tailor the dialogue to the drawings, using words to make the points I couldn't show in the pictures. This also forces me to write less and make my words count. When it comes to dialogue, less is more. In each balloon, I try to make my point as briefly as I can, and I avoid *telling* a reader something I can *show* with a drawing.

Scripting and lettering a page for *Quantum Mechanics* took anywhere from a half hour to three hours (not counting re-writes!), depending on how much characters had to say. A discussion scene like the one below obviously took longer to script than an action scene.

I do my lettering and word balloons on a computer (like most folks in the comics business these days). Good thing, too—I'm terrible at hand lettering!

Heaven's in the Details: Inking

Finishing the artwork in ink is the most time-consuming part of the job, and for me, the most fun. This is where I really start to see my drawings come alive, and where precision and accuracy count. What you lay down in black is what goes on the printed page, so every mark is meaningful.

I used Micron pens and a sable brush for inking *Quantum Mechanics*. Inking a page of *Quantum Mechanics* usually took three to four hours, depending on how complicated it was.

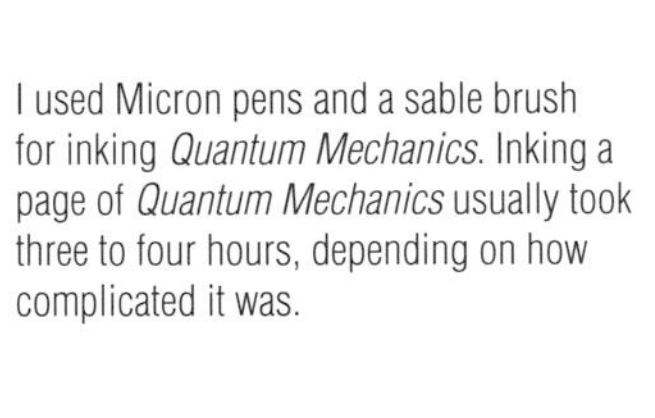

The Finishing Touch: Coloring

Quantum Mechanics, like almost all comics these days, was colored on the computer. I did most of the work in a program called Manga Studio (an older version of what is now called Clip Studio Paint), often adding finishing touches and digital effects in Photoshop.

Modern comic book coloring can get pretty complicated. Some books look like they were practically *painted* digitally.

I kept the coloring for *Quantum Mechanics* pretty simple. I used mostly solid colors, adding only a few color blends where needed, and finishing with some simple shadows and highlights to add depth and a sense of lighting. I took this approach for two reasons: I thought it fit the cartoony nature of the art better than fancy digital painting would, and I wanted to finish the book sometime this decade! Coloring took about two hours a page.

▲ *A screenshot from my computer of a finished color page in Manga Studio (a.k.a. Clip Studio Paint).*

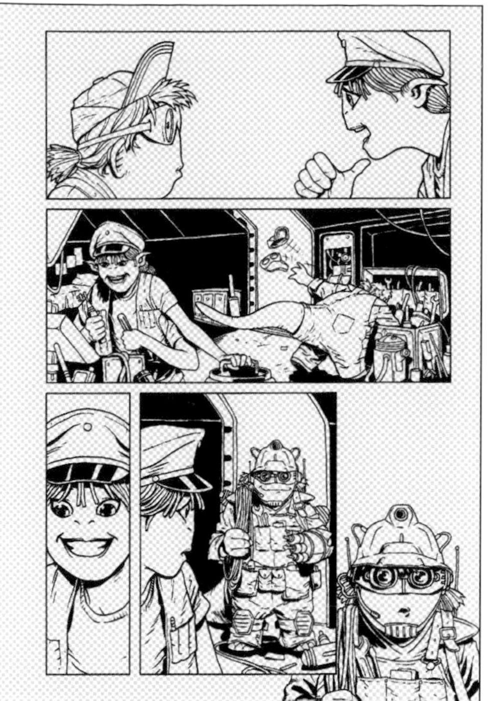

▲ I scan inked artwork and bring it into the coloring program with no background (the absence of a white background is indicated by those gray checks).

▲ I start by dropping in whatever I think will be the main background color, then filling in the margins and spaces between panels with white.

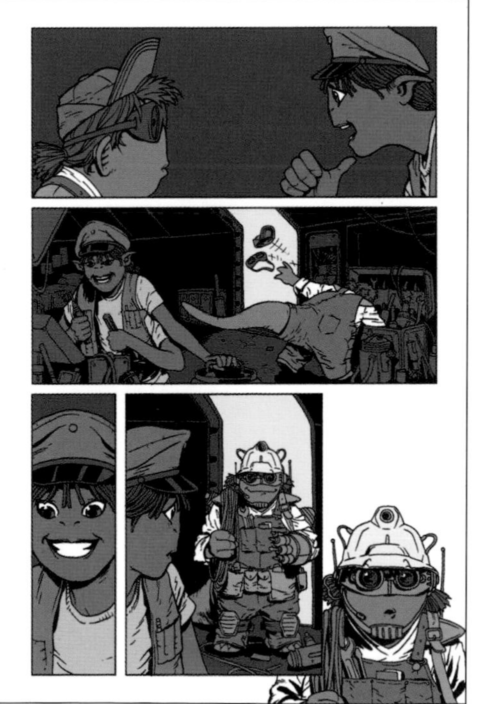

▲ Next, I lay in flat colors—no blends or special effects yet. I know if my flats don't look good, no amount of computer wizardry will save the page from being ugly.

▲ Once I'm satisfied with the flat color, then I add gradients where I think they'll help, then some highlights (as seen above), and some shadowing (as seen on the previous page).

Cover Me: Creating a Cover

Whoever said you can't judge a book by its cover never worked in publishing. Customers in book stores *always* judge a book by its cover before they even pick it up off the shelf. So what goes on the front gets special attention.

The image on the right-hand page is the cover I created as part of the proposal to publishers. (Notice the look of Rox and Zam reflects those early sketches you saw on page 212.) Everyone loved it, but at some point the Lion Forge folks realized it didn't get the main appeal of the story across: too steampunk, and no pirates or spaceships!

The sketches (with some digital effects) on this page show the process we went through to solve those problems and create what you see on the front of this book. More spaceship, less spaceship, no pirates, lots of pirates—these are the sorts of exercises you go through to create a cover that will attract readers' attention.

ISBN: 978-1-941302-66-8

Library of Congress Control Number: 2018932768

Printed in China.

10 9 8 7 6 5 4 3 2 1